WILD IRISH RENEGADE

BOOK 11 IN THE MYSTIC COVE SERIES

TRICIA O'MALLEY

LOVEWRITE PUBLISHING

WILD IRISH RENEGADE
The Mystic Cove Series
Book Eleven

Editor:
Jena O'Connor

"Trust in dreams, for in them is hidden the gate to eternity." – Khalil Gibran

CHAPTER 1

"Watch it!" Niamh Kearney shouted, but it was too late. Like seeing a horror movie in slow motion, she stared in shock as an entire cup of coffee – not hers, either – toppled over and soaked her ancient laptop. It just showed how distracted she was by the presence of the coffee-spiller, none other than William "Mac" Macgregor himself, that she hadn't used her powers to stop the cup from spilling before it destroyed her computer. The computer which held the proposal she was meant to submit to her professor next week for a home-based study on the science and myths of telekinesis. The proposal that would lead to her thesis that would lead to her graduation, a year early, from University.

"Oh shite, I've gone and made a mess of things, haven't I?" Mac grabbed napkins and began to mop up the table while cameras flashed around them. Heat flooded Niamh's cheeks, and she turned away from the cameras, knowing a red flush would be tinging her porcelain skin. She wished she was one of those women who could get angry or upset without it showing acutely on her face, but alas, that was not one of her gifts. The last thing she wanted was to have her furious face looking like a bright red apple splashed across all the gossip magazines.

And one thing was certain – where Mac went, the paparazzi followed. He was Ireland's rugby star, a god among men, a fantasy to women, and right now? An absolute annoyance to Niamh. She wanted him, his fake-contrite expression, and his cameras away from her – *now*.

"Just stop!" Niamh hissed as he awkwardly patted her laptop with napkins dripping in coffee. "You've ruined my computer and I had critical documents on it."

"Can't you just retrieve them from the cloud?" Mac asked and then winced when she severed him with a look.

"I don't have the cloud on this computer. It's ancient. But it's reliable. Well, it was until you came along to preen for the cameras and decided to murder it."

"Ouch," Mac said, holding a hand to his chest. His very muscular chest, which Niamh was refusing to notice – so she told herself. The man was built like a tank. Tall, broad shouldered, and rippling through with thick muscles, Mac exuded charm and deadly strength in equal amounts. People instinctively moved out of the way when he walked into a room and then immediately turned back when they realized who he was. Now, the entire coffee shop, including the women who had stopped to take photos with him, watched the debacle unfold with bated breath.

Niamh loved her little corner coffee shop, Bee & Bun, as it had a long-standing tradition of combining modern aesthetics with the comforts of home. She'd spent many hours here, tucked behind the little alcove in the back room, staring into the fire as she worked through one complicated hypothesis or another in her head.

"Just go on with yourself. I need to clean this up." Niamh smiled a quick thanks to James, part-owner of the café, when he brought several dry towels for her to use.

"I'd get that in a bag of rice quickly," James advised as he gave Mac an aggrieved look before returning to the counter.

"Why would you put it in rice?" Mac asked, grabbing one of the towels before Niamh could stop him. He began to wipe each individual key of her keyboard, and for a moment Niamh was transfixed by his powerful hands and how they moved softly over the keys. Would he be that gentle with a woman?

Shaking her head, she looked up at him as she patted the towel across her soaked pants.

"Rice is meant to soak up the moisture. It's not a fail-proof way to save your electronics, but sometimes it works. Sure, and I can't believe you haven't heard of this before. Haven't you ever dropped your phone in water then?"

"I just buy a new one." Mac shrugged as though it was the easiest thing in the world.

"Well, now, isn't that nice? I guess not all of us can afford to replace our electronics every week like yourself." As a few of Mac's women giggled at her, Niamh shoved back from the table. She wasn't going to be made to feel like some pauper because she took care of things that mattered to her. "Just stop. I'll take care of this."

"Hey, I really am sorry. The least I can do is buy you a new computer." Mac held a hand to his heart, giving her a soft smile combined with puppy dog eyes. It was highly effective, and Niamh imagined it had worked with thousands of women through the years. With golden-brown hair, sparkling blue eyes, and a wide grin, Mac's face was made for magazines which was why he was the paparazzi's darling. His photos sold well, and millions of women sighed over his antics each week in the gossip columns.

"What you can do is leave me alone. You've given me enough trouble for the day." Niamh leveled him with a look that dared him to challenge her. The moment drew out between them as he took her measure and realized just how upset she was.

"I understand. Again, I'm truly sorry."

For a moment, Niamh saw past the flash of his exterior to the man within. She'd learned enough about reading people with some of her extra-sensory gifts that she knew he wasn't lying. The man *was* contrite. It was just that he couldn't help being who he was – a filthy rich and incredibly famous rugby star. Life was just easier for people like that; doors opened for them, and new computers were a dime a dozen.

Different worlds, Niamh told herself as she wrapped her computer in the towels and shoved it into her bag. Just because they came from different worlds didn't mean he was inherently a bad person – just a clumsy one.

"No bother. I'll get it sorted out."

"Can I buy you a coffee or something?" Mac asked, as she went to move past him. Niamh paused. Though he wasn't exceptionally tall, Niamh had not been blessed in the height department. Forced to look up at him, she just shook her head.

"No, Mac. I don't need anything from you."

"I know you don't. I can tell you're the type of woman who takes care of herself. But perhaps you're wanting a cup of coffee with me? Not needing?" The easy charm again, which Niamh was sure had worked for him count-less times. It slid over her, enticing her to take a moment with one of the most famous men in Ireland, but she resisted.

"I don't need, or want, a cup of coffee with you. What I want to do is go see if I can fix my laptop before I lose my work."

"That's fair. Can I at least get your name?"

"If I give you my name, will you stop blocking my way?"

Immediately Mac moved out of her way, and Niamh was surprised to see a faint flash of embarrassment in his eyes.

"I didn't realize I was blocking you. My apologies, again."

"My name is Niamh. I really must be going."

"Good luck with the computer, Niamh. If it doesn't work, here's my private number. Call me and I'll get you a new computer. I promise." Niamh hesitated at the card he held out to her, but not wanting to feel like a complete bitch, she took it and tucked it in her bag.

"I won't be calling you. But I appreciate the gesture." With that, Niamh strode past the women who were now glaring at her, having seen Mac pass her his card, and turned her head from the cameras pointed in her direction.

At the very least, Niamh was grateful she hadn't come to the coffee shop in her leggings and baggy jumper that day. Instead, knowing she had a meeting later, she'd donned leather joggers, slouchy suede boots, and a black sweater with gold zippers on the arms. Fashion was a love for her, but Niamh almost exclusively thrifted her clothes. While her parents insisted they could help her through Uni, Niamh had wanted to do it on her own. It was nice knowing she had the support if needed, but it was more important for her to make it on her own.

Which meant she'd have to dip into her meager savings if she couldn't fix the laptop. Sighing, she left Bee & Bun and pulled out her phone to look up the nearest computer repair shop.

It was going to be a long day.

CHAPTER 2

*T*he next morning, Niamh returned to Bee & Bun early to secure her favorite spot under the alcove by the small fireplace. She'd need extra espresso shots to finish the amount of work that faced her today. The word was still out on whether her laptop would live to see another day, but the tech guy had been kind enough to pull her documents from the hard drive for her and she'd been able to print out her proposal. Now, she would have to make her notes longhand and secure some time at the computer lab later to finish it up.

Niamh was trying really hard not to be angry about the demise of her laptop. It wasn't the laptop really, as the computer was on its last legs, but it was the fact that she had been steadily working toward this proposal and was equal parts nervous and excited for how her professor was going to receive it. She'd lucked out in finding an open-minded mentor who was willing to explore the science behind certain parapsychology phenomenon, particularly telekinesis. Niamh hadn't quite worked up the courage to admit she actually had this particular ability. Her goal was to do a study, with herself as a subject, and report to her professor various measurables and refer to the subject of the study as anonymous. Niamh wasn't sure how her professor would respond to keeping the subject anonymous, but it wasn't an unheard-of tactic in the scientific community. She'd simply assign a code of numbers to the subject and continue on with her assessment. The reason she wanted to pull the research off campus was simple – Niamh didn't want anyone walking in or observing her experiments.

She'd spent enough time feeling like she didn't fit in anywhere while growing up. Sure, she'd had a loving family and a few tight girlfriends, and that was more than a girl could ask for, really. But she'd learned that the touch of otherness that clung to her made some people skittish around her. Niamh tried to compensate for that by being overly friendly, which sometimes could be a problem in her industry. However, irrespective of the fact that she was in male-dominated classes at Uni, Niamh never tried to downplay her looks or shrink from answering a question. With lush auburn hair, moody grey eyes, and a generous mouth, she'd been called everything from a Siren to a seductress. She was aware, in a cerebral sense, that she was beautiful, but it meant nothing more to her than that. Her face was her face, her body was her body, but there were much more interesting things to talk about than who was prettiest. Like why some people were able to see auras around humans while others were not?

"Isn't she a lovely one this morning?" James stopped

by her table with a warm scone and a cup of clotted cream on a small Robin's-egg blue plate.

"Oh? This old thing?" Niamh held out her arm dramatically and they both appreciated the fringe that fell from the sleeves of her vintage 70s-style bohemian dress she'd paired with a thick leather wrap belt and chunky military-style boots. "Actually, quite literally this old thing. Sure, and I was lucky the day I found it at the vintage shop just down the road from here."

"Sometimes they have the best stuff. Didn't I score that eighties-style leather bomber jacket from there?"

"You did at that. A great piece."

"Listen, love. I hate to be doing this, but I'd rather you see it from me." A quick look of sympathy crossed James's face and Niamh stiffened. She realized now he held something behind his back.

"Give it to me." Niamh held out her hand, though she already knew what was coming her way.

"I mean, in all fairness, it paints him in a bad light for ruining your computer."

"I look awful, don't I?"

"You look lovely, you always do. But just a touch furious. I think the press is enjoying a woman not being wowed by Mac for once, is all."

"Dublin Beauty rejects Mac after he destroys her computer," Niamh read out loud. For a moment she winced at the image, where her face mirrored that of a stone-cold Medusa, and then reminded herself she was a scientist and not some society It-girl. Niamh scanned the article quickly and then glanced back up at James.

"That's good press for you, James. They mentioned the café."

James, relieved she wasn't upset, nodded happily. "I'm sorry, as I know you like to keep a low profile, but this is going to be killer for the café. Speaking of which, I need to be getting back to the counter now. Wave if you need anything. Scone's on me, doll."

"Thanks. I'll take another espresso next round you make."

"On it."

Niamh sighed and ripped a corner off the scone, dunking it in the cream before munching thoughtfully. She really didn't want to be bothered by the silly gossip article. And what had James meant when he said she liked to keep a low profile? Niamh wasn't even aware she *had* a profile. She just liked to come in and do her work and move on with her day. Granted, she often had to field conversations from the men who frequently stopped at her table, so maybe that was what James had been referring to? Shaking her head, she picked up her pen and immediately dropped it when someone appeared at her table. A very large and unwelcome someone.

"Good morning, Niamh. I was hoping to see you again today." Mac, dressed in a bright blue jumper that made his eyes pop and simple denim pants, smiled brightly from where he'd stopped by her side. He stood a few feet back, a bag in one hand, and raised his other hand cautiously. "I'll just stand over here to avoid accidently destroying something else of yours."

Niamh turned and scanned the busy café to see all eyes on them again, but thankfully no paparazzi. It must have been too early for them to get out of bed. In fact, she was surprised Mac was up this early, what with his hard-partying reputation.

"That might be best. In fact, you could take a few more steps back, and then a few more, and then find yourself out the door." Niamh smiled sweetly at him to take some of the sting out of her words.

"Och, you wound me. May I?" Mac indicated the chair across from her.

"Mac, I really am busy."

"I promise I won't take up more than say…fifteen minutes of your time. I'll even set a timer."

Sighing, Niamh thought about it. The man clearly felt bad about the day before and she wondered if he would keep showing up until he could make whatever amends he needed to make to not feel guilty. And maybe just a small part of her was enjoying looking at him.

"Go ahead."

"I set the timer." Mac held up his phone and showed it to her and placed it on the table before easing into the bistro-style chair. Niamh barely suppressed a giggle. He was so large that he looked like he was sitting at a little girl's play tea party table.

"What's so funny?"

"I…I was just thinking how the world must not be built for men of your size."

"Sure, and it's not always comfortable, I'll admit it." Mac grinned and looked around the room. She wondered if he even saw how people watched him anymore. "It's why I bought this massive comfortable chair for my living room.

I can just relax into it at the end of a long day and not worry that a leg's going to break off."

Niamh was shocked when an image of her curling up on his lap in that comfortable chair flickered through her mind. Pushing that quickly aside, she pasted a polite smile on her face.

"What can I do for you then?"

"I came to apologize to you and bring you a gift. I hope you'll be accepting it so I don't have to feel like I've ruined…well whatever it was you were working on."

"You didn't." Niamh indicated the pages in front of her on the table. "The repair tech was able to grab my documents for me."

"Well, that's a relief, isn't it?" Mac let out a big sigh as though he'd actually been up all night worrying about it.

"Therefore, I don't need your gift."

"Perhaps you'll accept it anyway?"

Niamh sighed and then held out her hand for the bag. Pulling out the tissue she found a slim laptop box holding a brand-new computer. Her mouth dropped open and she looked at Mac askance.

"Mac, I can't possibly be accepting this."

"No, you must. See I didn't even go and buy the newest or the fanciest one. I could surmise you were someone who held onto things for a while and valued your belongings. The sales guy assured me this is like a good sturdy workhorse. Should be lasting you years if clumsy jocks like me don't douse it in coffee."

Niamh raised her eyebrows at Mac's use of the word "surmise." She'd had him pegged for a dumb jock who cared more about sport and fast women than he did educa-tion. Perhaps she would need to revise her opinion.

Niamh's gaze fell on the article in front of her again.

"You aren't just doing this so you look good in the press, are you?"

Shock crossed Mac's face and his mouth dropped open. Genuine shock— that, Niamh could read.

"Those arseholes? They're always following me. The team's publicist loves it and tells me to make nice with them. But they drive me crazy. It's why I came by early today. I figured none of them would be up this early and I could give you this in private." Mac looked around at the crowded café, the patrons all staring at them and shook his head. "Well, as private as I can be, I suppose."

Niamh struggled with what to do. On one hand, she really did need a computer, and he *had* been the one to damage hers. On the other, she was a strong, independent woman who could take care of herself. And, glancing down at the computer model, she knew she wouldn't be able to afford a laptop this nice – not to mention it would be really helpful for her experiments. With a small smile, Niamh met his eyes.

"Well, then. Thank you. I really shouldn't accept this, but it will be quite useful for my study."

"I'd love to hear more about that study. Perhaps over dinner?" Mac leaned in, tilting his head and looking up at her with big eyes and a hopeful smile.

"Oh, I'm sure that look has worked for you a thousand times." Niamh let out a peal of laughter that had Mac leaning back, affronted.

"It wasn't a look. It's just *how* I look."

"Oh, it's a look. Mac, come on. You can't play me. I can read your little playboy act from a mile away." Niamh continued to chuckle and then stilled when she saw a flash of vulnerability in his eyes. "I'm just having you on a bit."

"I know, I get it. Everyone thinks I'm only out to score. Both on the pitch and with women."

"Well, wasn't that what you were after here?" Niamh pointed out.

"I asked you to dinner. Not to bed. One doesn't automatically equal the other. There's a lot of steps that need to happen between the two." Mac shook his head and Niamh realized he was honestly aggrieved.

"That's fair. You are correct, you did just ask me for dinner. I shouldn't have made that jump. It's not right to make assumptions."

"Thank you." The smile that warmed Mac's face was a real one this time and Niamh felt her resolve weaken.

"And just for that, I'll have dinner with you."

"You will?" Mac's eyes lit up as the timer on his phone sounded. He immediately turned it off and stood, respecting their bargain.

"Timer's gone off. I suggest you leave before you delay my work any further and I'm unable to meet you for dinner."

"I'm already gone. You have my number. Text me for directions later." With that, Mac zipped from the café and everyone turned to watch him go. In seconds, James was at her table with another espresso, his eyes wide.

"I wanted to bring this to you when he was here, but the conversation looked intense. Did he..." James's eyes fell on the laptop box. "Bring you a new computer?"

"Sure and he did. The scum," Niamh said lightly.

"Absolute bastard," James agreed, pressing his lips tightly together as he put the espresso on the table and patted her shoulder.

"I'm having dinner with him."

"Of course you are. You'd be a fool not to."

CHAPTER 3

*B*y the time dinnertime came around, Niamh had barely enough time to get ready for their date. Because Mac had given her virtually zero information on where they were going or what they were doing, she defaulted to her standard foolproof date-night outfit. Not that she dated much. Niamh tried to remember her last date as she pulled on figure-hugging leather pants, a silky scoop-necked top in deep maroon, and heeled boots. Clipping large hoop earrings in, she smudged some makeup around her eyes and left her hair to tumble wildly around her shoulders. Right, she'd gone out with the lad from her psychology class. He'd been…well, perfectly alright she supposed. But there'd been no spark of interest on her end, and she'd resisted his advances at the end of the night.

Snagging her vintage faded leather jacket and a dainty purse, Niamh left her small studio apartment and clattered down the stairs. She'd been lucky to find this place and at a rent she could easily afford on her wages from working part-time at the library. Tucked on the top floor of a four-story walk-up close to the university, her apartment afforded her the solitude she craved, and she'd created a little oasis for herself there. Niamh loved bringing the outside in, and an abundance of plants and fresh flowers mixed with eclectic lamps and vintage movie posters combined to make her place feel welcoming. Plus, it allowed her to practice her powers in relative peace as she worked to figure out a way to measure what she could do with science.

Her family would say to accept that it was magick. It had been passed down through their blood from the waters of Grace's Cove that were enchanted by her ancestor, Grace O'Malley. Niamh had always accepted this story. However, what she really wanted to do was figure out if there was a way to define magick in a way that could be understood or even replicated. Perhaps it was like capturing lightning in a bottle, but at the very least it was fascinating to her.

Niamh drew up short at the flashy Porsche parked by the curb in front of her building. The car was a screaming orange color, and Mac leaned lazily against the hood and signed autographs while he waited for her. When he saw Niamh, a smile lit his face and he straightened, pushing through the crowd to go to her. A few people held their phones up to take pictures and Niamh immediately kicked herself for not spending more time on her hair and makeup.

No, Niamh lectured herself. Don't fall into that trap. Lead with your brains, not your looks.

"You look stunning," Mac said. He reached out to hook an arm through hers, seeming to sense she was uncomfortable with the crowd that had gathered, and quickly ushered her through the people. Settling her into the car, he hopped in and revved the engine before zipping quickly away from the curb.

"Does that happen everywhere you go?" Niamh asked, turning to watch the crowd take photos of his car as they left.

"Pretty much." The way he said it was as though he was expecting her to be impressed and Niamh instantly wondered if she'd made a mistake going on this date with him. Turning back, she studied his profile as he drove competently through the busy streets of Dublin. Tonight he wore dark grey pants, a fitted black sweater, and a leather jacket. He looked confident, sleek, and just a little dangerous. The combination shouldn't have appealed to Niamh, and yet a touch of heat flooded her cheeks. Turning away, she looked out the window.

"Sure and that has to get annoying."

"Actually, it does. And it doesn't." Mac paused as he considered his words. "When it's fans – I like to be taking the time. Because I have a responsibility as a role model to do that. Without the fans, we are nothing, really. So, if stopping to chat with someone who loves rugby because it takes them away from everyday life, or a little boy who hopes to become a player one day? Yeah, that's worth it to me then. But for the rest who just want to be near a celebrity? Nah, that's annoying. Plus, a lot of people forget I am human."

"What do you mean by that?" Niamh laughed.

"Well, I mean, think about this – if you were just having a wee wander down the road and someone jumped in your face with their phone to take a selfie without asking permission of you first – how would you be feeling then?"

"I'd…yeah, sure and I'd be a bit heated about it now, wouldn't I?" Niamh considered the scenario.

"Exactly. People don't stop to ask if I want my picture taken. There's no…oh I just want to pop into the store for some ice cream. You're always thinking about what you're wearing or what you're doing. What you're reading…what brand you're wearing…it's kind of messing with me mind at times."

"I never thought about it that way. You seem so comfortable in all the pictures of you."

Mac pulled the car into the valet of a restaurant. The building was all sleek glass and flashy lighting, and Niamh wondered if this was one of those places that would bring out the tiniest portion of food on massive plates. She certainly hoped not, as she was famished after her busy day. Smiling her thanks to the valet who opened her door, she waited as Mac rounded the car and slid his arm through hers again.

His nearness unsettled Niamh. He was such a large presence – both physically and charismatically – that she felt almost overpowered by him. A ripple of awareness shot through her when he was close, and Niamh wasn't sure what to make of it exactly.

"Mr. Macgregor, we have your table waiting." The host, in a smart velvet green suit coat, took their coats and then led them through the restaurant to a private room in the back. The restaurant was done up in all sharp spikey chandeliers, clear acrylic tables, and huge pop-art pieces on the wall. It was funky, Niamh thought, but lacked the warmth she liked in some of her favorite restaurants. The clear chairs and tables were a bold choice, but Niamh realized this was a place where people liked to see and be seen. What better way to scrutinize another woman's outfit than to see right through the table?

"Good evening." A waiter materialized by their table and Niamh started as he laid a napkin across her lap. Mac winked at her, and she flushed, realizing she'd given away the fact that she didn't eat in fancy establishments such as this one often.

"Champagne for the lady?" The waiter held up a bottle. Niamh didn't know labels, but she assumed it was ridiculously expensive and if they opened the bottle then they would have to pay for the whole bottle. Instead, she shook her head slightly.

"Yellow Spot whiskey, please. Neat."

Mac raised an eyebrow at her, but the waiter merely smiled.

"Of course, and for you, sir?"

"Sparkling water with a lime please."

"Do you not drink?" Niamh asked him after the waiter had left.

"Not if I am driving. And I have an early training session. I want to have a clear head."

"Ah, I'm surprised. I suppose I shouldn't be believing everything I read in the press." Niamh looked up and nodded her thanks when the waiter delivered their drinks.

"First course will arrive shortly."

"Oh…are we not looking at the menu?" Niamh looked around.

"They offer a five-course meal option. It seemed to have a little bit of everything on it, so I thought I couldn't go wrong. If you don't like anything, I'll be happy to order you something else."

"Right, sure, that sounds grand then." Why not give it a go? It annoyed her just a bit that he hadn't let her order, but at least he hadn't picked out one dish for her, instead providing her with several options to choose from.

"So, you're reading up on me?" Mac smiled at her, and Niamh's brain scrambled as she tried to remember what they had been talking about.

"Oh, the press? I mean, it's hard not to be seeing it, no? It feels like you're in columns every day. Out partying hard, lots of women, lavish lifestyle..." Niamh glanced around at the restaurant they were in and shrugged a shoulder.

"Don't believe everything you read, Niamh. The press is going for the shot they think will sell to the mags. That's it. It isn't always a true portrayal of my life."

"Okay, then...tell me. What does your life look like? Because so far..." Niamh gestured with her whiskey glass at the restaurant. "It's living up to the magazines. You know...fancy restaurants that serve miniscule portions. That kind of thing."

"What's wrong with this place?" Mac looked around in confusion.

"I didn't say anything was wrong." Niamh quieted as the waiter returned with their first dish – what looked to be a singular piece of cheese with a walnut and some sauce drizzled on it.

They both looked down at their plates and then up at each other before bursting into laughter.

"I think you've got me on this one, Niamh. Tell me… what are you really in the mood for?" Mac leaned over the table, humor in his eyes.

"I could go for a cheeseburger and chips."

Mac stood and left the room, giving Niamh a moment to gather her thoughts. He was a good sport, she realized, and not afraid to take charge when needed. Filing those facts away, she smiled at him when he returned.

"The chef has promised the best cheeseburger in Dublin for you this evening. In fact, I think he was quite delighted by the request."

"He's probably used to all the models picking at his food." Niamh laughed.

"I have a confession to make…" Mac looked around and then leaned in, his voice a whisper. "I always stop at a chippie on the way home after I eat here."

"Scandalous!" Niamh laughed.

"I'm a big lad, I need a lot of food."

"So, tell me, aside from consuming a lot of food, what do you do all day?" Niamh relaxed into her chair, happy to know real food was on the way out and looked across at Mac. She wanted to get a better read on him, and she let her mind go a little loose so she could just see the faint tinges of his aura surrounding him.

"When we are in season? Mad busy. I'm training, giving press conferences, working plays with the team, traveling…"

"And in down season?" He had a nice blue aura with

lovely hints of gold, Niamh was surprised to see. So maybe not as ego-driven as she had first assumed.

"I still train, for I don't want to lose my edge. But I have more time. I can actually have a social life, or work on sponsorship deals, travel to places I want to go…that kind of thing."

"Sponsorship deals? Sounds fancy."

"They can be lucrative. It's another way to make money from a career that has a short timeline." An indeterminable look crossed Mac's face before he offered her a smile again. Niamh wondered if he was worried about what his life would look like after rugby.

"Make hay while the sun shines?" Niamh asked. The waiter entered bearing their plates as though he was presenting the finest dishes in all the land. Niamh was pleased to see her plate was overflowing with perfectly cooked chips and a mammoth burger. Her mouth watered in anticipation.

"Now, this is more like it." Mac looked equally as excited for real food. "Let's dig in."

For a moment, they ate in companionable silence, and Niamh was happy to discover that the chef really did know what he was doing. When the edge of hunger had vanished, she leaned back and saluted Mac with her whiskey.

"This hits the spot."

"I'm ordering this every time I come here now." Mac grinned at her. "Tell me, Niamh – what were you working on that I nearly destroyed the other day?"

Deciding to test him a bit to see how much of a skeptic

he was, Niamh met his eyes and opened her senses to read him better.

"It's a proposal about doing a study on parapsychology. Particularly telekinesis, but also other parapsychology phenomenon. I want to know if there are scientific ways to measure the energy produced in said phenomenon and if it could be replicated elsewhere."

Mac stilled and Niamh was shocked to feel a pulse of vulnerability wash across the table at her. That was...odd, Niamh thought. Quickly, Mac shifted the emotion and raised his eyebrows.

"That sounds intense. But also, deeply fascinating. Is this for your degree then?"

"Yes, my masters."

"Where would you take something like this...like what do you see for a career for yourself?"

"Ideally? I'd like to be helping children who experience such phenomenon. Help them to understand or adjust to those extra abilities. It can be scary for them, growing up and not understanding where these powers are coming from."

"But...then that means you believe these extrasensory abilities are not only real, but that there are enough people experiencing them that you can make a career from it?"

"Absolutely." Niamh met his look of disbelief dead on. "Ever heard of specializing? My services will be in high demand, have no doubt about that."

"I'm...well, I'm intrigued, I have to admit. It sounds like magic."

"It might well be," Niamh laughed and leaned back, taking another sip of her whiskey. "But I'd like to be at least given the chance to define or measure it in other ways."

"Good luck to you then. I'll be interested to hear how it goes for you."

On the way out of the restaurant after dinner, Niamh grew impatient as Mac was stopped at every table to shake hands, sign an autograph, or talk about some meeting or another. Didn't the man know how to say no? All the warm feelings she'd been building up toward him quickly dissolved when they walked out into an explosion of flashes from the paparazzi's cameras. Niamh held her hand up to shade her eyes, as the bright lights against the darkness of night nearly blinded her. It was in that instant she realized, no matter how charming Mac had seemed at dinner, this was not a life she craved. It was too fast, too fancy, and much too public for the work she wished to pursue. Sighing, because for a moment the fantasy of quiet and studious Niamh dating a famous rugby star had excited her, she knew she had to get back to reality.

"Shall we…" Mac looked over at her once they were in the car, allowing her to make the next move.

"Please take me home, Mac. I've had a long day and I have an even longer one tomorrow."

"Of course." Though Niamh registered his flash of disappointment, she figured he'd get over it quickly with the next leggy blonde that threw herself at him. There had been at least five in the restaurant who would have eagerly signed up for the role.

When he pulled to a stop at her apartment, he immediately got out and rounded the hood to open her door.

"Oh, you don't have to…" Niamh trailed off as he took her hand.

"It's dark out. I'll see you safely to your door."

"Thank you." Once they'd climbed the steps to the front door of her apartment building, Niamh turned and looked up at him. The night was brisk, and she shivered a bit in her coat – though she couldn't be sure if it was from his nearness or the cold.

"Can I see you again? I'd like to, if you're interested." Mac's eyes were hopeful.

"Thank you for a lovely dinner, Mac. I…I'm sorry, but I really think it is best if we're just friends." Her heart fell at the sadness that flitted into his eyes. Leaning up she pressed a soft kiss to his cheek, though her heart urged her to do more. "Thank you again for the best cheeseburger I've had in ages."

"Of course. Just friends? You're certain?" Mac raised an eyebrow at her.

"Yes, I'm certain."

"I'll be seeing you around, Niamh. You can always call me if you need anything." Mac turned and made his way to his car. Niamh imagined a lot of women took him up on that offer, but she wasn't going to be one of them.

"Safe home…" With that, Niamh closed the door behind her and for a moment just leaned against it, her heart hammering in her chest, her mind whirling with all the what-ifs. The biggest one being – what if she'd just turned her back on something really great?

CHAPTER 4

"*W*ell, now, this is getting creepy." Niamh gave Mac a look when he showed up at her table at Bee & Bun the next morning.

"I thought you said we could be friends?" Mac smiled, a hopeful look on his face. He was dressed in a track suit and she assumed he must have come from his training that he'd told her about.

"Wouldn't a friend text and ask to join for coffee then?"

"I guess so. But I just got out of practice and I have a few contracts to look over while I shove as much food in my face as I can. I heard the food here is good. How was I to know you'd be here again? Unless you come here every day?"

"No, I don't come here every day. Just when I'm busy or before a work shift." Niamh took a deep breath, ignoring the little tug of joy she felt at seeing him and waved a hand to the chair across from her. "Go on, then. Make yourself at home."

"See? Friends." Mac beamed at her and then shared that same smile with James when he arrived with a full Irish breakfast. James nearly dropped the plate at the full force of Mac's smile and shot Niamh a look.

"I'll have another coffee, please. And a cinnamon scone if any are left."

"No problem." James gave her a look promising they would talk later, and Niamh bit back a smile.

Mac dug into his food with enthusiasm, and Niamh's heart did a funny little twist in her chest as she watched him. What would it be like to share breakfast with this man every day?

"How was training?"

"Ah, it was good at that. I'm a bit sore from tweaking a quad muscle last week. But I'll work through it." Mac shrugged. "The one thing that's certain about rugby is you'll always be getting hurt one way or the other. You should see my bruises when I'm in season. I look like a brawler."

"Charming, I'm sure…" Niamh leaned back, studying him. He certainly looked like a man who could handle a few bruises, but she had to imagine the repeated battering he took had to do a number on him. "Do you have any lingering injuries or have you been able to heal up?"

"Knock on wood." Mac rapped the table lightly. "Thus far, I've been just fine. It won't always be that way, the older I get."

"Do rugby players often retire because of injuries? Or because of old age? What is old age in rugby? I confess I don't really know much about the sport…" Niamh laughed when Mac looked at her in shock. "What? You've never met someone who doesn't follow rugby?"

"Not in Ireland, no. What is it you do with your free time then?"

"Um, sure and you have to know there's other things to life than sports?" Niamh raised an eyebrow at Mac and then laughed when he made a play of being confused by her question.

"I can't say that I do…nope." Niamh blinked as Mac finished his breakfast. That had to be a record, she thought. The man was hungry. She smiled her thanks to James who returned with her coffee and scone.

"Well, that looks smashing. I'll have one as well when you're getting a chance."

"Sure thing, Mac." James said his name a little breathlessly, and Niamh rolled her eyes.

"Do you have that effect on everyone you meet?"

"What effect?" Mac looked up from where he was pulling out a folder from his bag.

"You really don't see it? The way people are nervous around you or like…worshipping?"

"I see it a bit. But I try not to. I'm just me, Niamh. I also happen to be very good at a sport that makes a ton of money. People seem to find that fascinating."

"Hmmm…" Niamh glanced down at where her phone vibrated on the table. She held up her finger for a moment and Mac nodded so she could take it.

"Hi, Mum, how's it going then?"

"What's this I hear about my daughter dating a famous celebrity? Your father's about to have an apoplectic fit.

Though I'm not sure if it is because it's some footballer or because he's worried for you."

"Rugby player, Mum." Niamh grinned when Mac held a hand to his chest with a wounded look on his face. "Would you like to speak to him? He's right here."

"Don't tell me you are in bed with him..." Niamh choked on a laugh when her father's voice replaced her mother's.

"Don't you dare say you are in bed with Mac."

"Hello, my brilliant and loving father. And thank you for inquiring into my sex life, but alas, I'm merely having a cup of coffee at my local shop here."

"Oh. Um..." Niamh could already see the brilliant red flush creeping up her father's cheeks. "Sorry about that. It's just...he's quite famous, you know."

"So I hear. Did you know you were famous, Mac?" Niamh grinned at him.

"Me? Is that right?" Mac laughed and held out his hand for her phone. Deciding to go with it, Niamh passed him the phone without warning her father.

"Hello, sir." Niamh realized he didn't know her last name.

"Mr. Kearney," Niamh whispered.

"Mr. Kearney. Nice to have a chat with you. Your daughter is a very kind and forgiving woman."

Warmth filled Niamh as Mac nodded his head as she was certain her father was delivering Mac a lecture.

"Of course, sir. Unfortunately for me, Niamh has told me we can only be friends, so I don't think you'll have to worry in that arena. But I'm holding her to it. I could use a good friend."

His words made her heart melt a bit. She suspected a man like him had a lot of people who wanted what he could offer – but didn't care about what he needed.

"Right, right. Of course. I'll be sure to do that. Ah, sure and that play's a tricky one. I'll work on it at next training. Right. Well, that sounds nice. No, I've never been to Grace's Cove."

Niamh's eyes widened, and she motioned for Mac to hand the phone back, but he just grinned at her.

"Is she coming home soon? For a few months? Well, now, maybe it would be nice to visit. I've never been to that area. A cracking pub, you say? Well, it's hard to resist that. Thanks for the invitation, Mr. Kearney. I'll be sure to let you know if I can make it down."

Niamh snatched the phone back, but her father had already disconnected.

"He seems nice. He cares a lot about you." Mac studied her with his striking blue eyes. A yearning seemed to coat his words.

"My parents are grand. They really are. I'm lucky to have them."

"Must be nice." Mac smiled his thanks when James returned with a cinnamon bun. Niamh's curiosity was piqued.

"Are you close with your family?"

"Nope. It's just my dad. Lost my mom at a young age. Dad cares most about how much money I can give him to go to the bookies."

"I'm sorry to hear that." Niamh meant it, too. She couldn't imagine not having the support that she did from her family. "No sisters or brothers?"

"Nope, just some cousins who use my name when it suits them." Mac didn't elaborate, but Niamh was beginning to get a picture. Everyone wanted a piece of Mac, but nobody seemed to give back to him. Despite not wanting to be a part of his flashy life, Niamh already knew that she wanted to help him. As friends, of course. The man was clearly lonely.

"You don't have to give anything to anyone, you know that right? You don't owe anyone."

"Ah, it's fine. It is what it is. Tell me…what's Grace's Cove like? Why are you going back for that long?" Change in subject there, Niamh noted, but let it slide.

"Well, if I get this proposal approved by my professor, I'll conduct the research at a lab there." Niamh didn't want to elaborate why, but Mac wasn't stupid, apparently.

"You know someone with extra-sensory abilities there, don't you?"

"I might," Niamh said.

"Maybe I could help you with your research? I could get out of town for a bit. Your father did invite me, after all."

"Really? And just how are you going to help me?" Niamh laughed. An odd look flashed into Mac's eyes, and he opened his mouth to speak, but then closed it. "I think I'll be just fine, Mac. I'm not certain my subjects would be comfortable with a famous person involved in the study. Many people are quite private with things like that."

"Sure, I understand. No bother." Mac shrugged a shoulder, but his energy didn't match his words. Why would he want to help her with schoolwork? Maybe he was lonelier than she realized.

"What contracts are you looking over today?" It was Niamh's turn to change the subject. She glanced at the time on her phone – she'd really need to finish her notes soon before she left for work.

"Two more sponsorship deals. I'm not sure if I want to do them."

"Why's that?" Intrigued, despite her time limit, Niamh tilted her head at him in question.

"Because one is for a dating app, and the other is for condoms."

"Ah…" Niamh thought about it for a moment. "I mean, the dating app seems a good fit, right?"

"What and condoms aren't?" Mac laughed when Niamh flushed.

"I just meant…you're on dates a lot."

"I don't need an app to get a date," Mac said, and Niamh rolled her eyes.

"Of course you don't. Women fall at your feet."

"Do you want me to lie or make some sound of protest here?" Mac asked, a cheeky grin on his face.

"Oh, you're impossible. Fine. Don't do the app but then do the condoms."

"That also seems awkward. Do I need to be discussing my sex life publicly?"

"A lot of it is already out there…" Niamh pointed out.

"Those are gossip rags, Niamh. I don't shag every girl I take to dinner." Mac looked pointedly at her, and she flushed again.

"Which is a good thing for us. Because it sounds like women come a little too easily for you. I'm not interested in being part of your buffet." Niamh glared at him and then looked down at her notes. "I really do need to finish this up."

"Fine, me too."

Silence descended on the table as they both worked on their notes, but Niamh was finding it particularly hard to focus on anything but Mac's presence. His energy seemed to fill the room, and her mind kept dancing over the fact that she could have helped him with a condom the night before if she'd chosen to. She'd certainly had a decidedly naughty dream featuring Mac and now those images played out in her mind. All those muscles…skin on skin…

Slamming her notebook closed, she stood abruptly, causing Mac to look up at her in surprise.

"Everything alright, then?"

"I have to go. Now," Niamh said awkwardly as she shoved her notebook into her tote.

"But you haven't finished your scone."

"You have it. Goodbye, Mac. I have to go to work. Good luck with your condoms and your dates." Niamh did a mental face palm and all but ran from the café, not daring to look back at where he sat.

"God, I'm an idiot…" Niamh hissed.

CHAPTER 5

*L*ater that day, Mac paced his penthouse apartment located on a quieter street in Dublin. He had too much energy today…in fact, he'd been restless ever since Niamh had made her comment about condoms and other women and then all but ran from the café. He'd ended up paying her bill, even though James had said it wasn't a bother as she was a regular at Bee & Bun.

He couldn't help but wonder if maybe she wasn't as unaffected by him as she proclaimed to be. God knew, he certainly wasn't unaffected by her. Niamh was…she was like a rose blossoming after the rain. Her face did little to hide her emotions, and Mac enjoyed the flush that would tinge her porcelain skin when she was embarrassed or angry.

Or aroused.

It had been impossible not to notice how her moody grey eyes had lingered on him that morning. He wanted to ask her what she'd really been thinking about when she'd stormed from their table. Mac wasn't sure why he cared so much what Niamh thought about him – but he did. She was different from all the other women he'd gone out with. Maybe she was different because she'd turned him down, but that wasn't what was drawing him to her. It was like she saw who he really was, well, at least as much as he was willing to show her.

There were things about himself that he shared with nobody.

He wondered, now, if she would be the one that he could share his secrets with. Maybe...but likely not. Becoming super-famous very quickly had brought a sharp learning curve for Mac with the main lesson being that he really could not trust anyone. The paparazzi loved a good scoop, and Mac knew that for a price anyone could be bought. Which is why he only showed the world what he wanted people to see. Mac would be ungrateful for his fame if it hadn't also brought some good along with it. Like the money and the opportunity to start working towards a secret dream of his – to run non-profit rugby clinics for kids in need. Rugby had saved him from hours of loneliness and neglect, so he was well aware the difference that a sport that some may call silly could have on child's life. He wasn't quite ready to launch the program yet, as he needed to oversee a lot more details, but Mac was still pleased that he'd at least gotten the ball rolling.

Still, he paced the house, restless. When his phone chimed with a text his first thought was of Niamh.

Hey mate, we're off to the club. Some Croatian models are here on a shoot.

For a moment, Mac hesitated. Normally, he would join his teammates and go party the night away. But now he thought about Niamh and how much he wanted to go to her apartment and cook dinner and talk about anything and nothing at all. But Mac knew he couldn't call her. Even if she did say they were friends, it would be just a touch too stalkerish of him if he hounded her. The poor woman needed some space from him, and she certainly wasn't at his beck and call.

You in?

Sighing, Mac went to his room to change. He had too much energy to sit at home tonight, so at the very least, maybe he could dance it off in the club and keep his mind off other things – like Niamh. Changing into dark jeans and a simple long-sleeved black t-shirt, Mac left his apartment and walked to the club. One of the benefits of living in Dublin was that he didn't have to drive anywhere if he didn't want to, but he did love having his Porsche in the city. Some days, when he felt this similar restless energy, he'd take off and drive for hours…just touring the coast or stopping in little villages along the way. Driving helped him focus, and if he had a problem, it often helped to sort things out.

Mac smiled at people who waved to him on the sidewalk but kept moving, not in the mood to sign autographs tonight. When he reached the club, the bouncer waved him right in past the line of people that snaked around the corner. Music pulsed, the bass hitting low in his stomach, and he took a deep breath before pasting a wide smile on his face as he went to meet his teammates. No, this wasn't his mood tonight, and his gut kept telling him to go home.

"Mate! Shots just lined up." Craig, one of his team-mates and generally a good guy, smacked him on the shoulder and passed him a shot glass of tequila. Despite how the press liked to showcase him as hard-partying, Mac rarely consumed more than a few drinks in an evening. He didn't like being out of control.

He didn't know what would happen if he ever was.

However, now, he accepted the shot easily and enjoyed the way the tequila trailed a hot path down his middle – warming his core. Turning around and leaning against the bar, Mac scanned the club.

"The models just left to go to the bathroom. What do they do in there together?" Craig pitched his voice over the music and leaned on the bar next to him.

Likely cocaine, Mac thought.

"Talk shit about men, of course. Did you hit on any yet?" Mac said instead.

"Nah, I'm waiting it out. John went in too eager and got shot down."

"Of course he did." Mac laughed. John was a rookie with an affable boy-next-door look that often worked for him, but not always.

"Fintan's here. With Kristie." Craig gave a subtle nod to where their team captain argued with his girlfriend in the corner. When she grabbed her purse and stormed to the bathroom, the men turned back to the bar before Fintan caught them staring.

"That looks to be going well," Mac said, and raised his finger to get a round of beers, knowing Fintan would likely be on his way over.

"He's going to propose, I guess." Craig shrugged.

"Is he? That's…a choice, I guess."

"What's a choice?" Fintan's voice said from behind them.

"Whether to get a leather couch for my living room," Mac said smoothly, turning to offer Fintan a smile. They'd never been close, but they were cordial. There was something about Fintan, a darkness that Mac shied away from. Maybe it was like recognizing like, but Mac wasn't interested in spending more time with learning about Fintan's problems. He had enough wounds as it was.

"It's durable," Fintan said. He nodded his thanks when Mac passed him a bottle of beer.

"Aye, it is at that."

"Not if you want to get a dog. They'll scratch it," Craig pointed out.

"Nah, buffs right out," Fintan argued.

"I'm not getting a dog," Mac said, taking a sip of his beer. The models returned from the bathroom, at least the women Mac assumed to be models. Rail thin, fake boobs, surreptitiously wiping at their noses. Mac wished the world would be kinder to women – particularly when it came to their bodies. Soft and round is the way he preferred them…like Niamh.

"Why not?" Fintan asked and Mac pulled his mind back from Niamh.

"Why what?"

"Why wouldn't you get a dog?"

"A dog needs a yard. Plus I'm gone a lot. What kind of life would that be for a pup?"

"If you got a girl, she'd watch the dog for you," Craig

pointed out. They all eyed the models who had made their way to the dance floor to pout and preen for the crowd.

"If I can't take care of a dog, what makes you think I can take care of a woman?" Mac laughed. "Both sound like way more responsibility than I'm interested in."

"Women are a fecking headache," Fintan groused. He rolled his eyes to where Kristie stood at the edge of the dance floor and scanned the room. "See ya later."

"Good luck." Craig winced when Fintan punched his arm.

"Come on, Mac. Be my wing-man?" Craig looked hopefully at him.

"Sure, why not?" At the very least, maybe some dancing would work out his restlessness. Together, they crossed the floor to the group of models.

Hours later, Mac was finally beginning to feel loose and like he'd burned off some of the angst that had been pinging around inside him all day. He'd danced with each model, and then a few other women on the dance floor, and now he was sweaty and feeling just a bit loose from the few drinks he'd had. This was his indicator that it was time to leave, as he preferred a happy buzz to help float him home.

Sliding his way to the bar, he nodded to the busy bartender who gave him a little salute. Mac had an account there and tipped the bartenders generously each month when he paid it up. Glancing at the long line that waited at the front door, Mac decided he wasn't up for it.

"I'm heading out the back," Mac called to the bartender. It wasn't uncommon for celebrities to sneak out the back way when things were too busy up front. The bartender nodded once more, Mac slipped past the bar and turned left at the hallway for the bathrooms. There, he slipped through another double set of doors and then through the exit door that was also monitored by a bouncer who just nodded to him as he passed through the door.

Once outside in the dimly lit alley, Mac took a deep breath of the cool night air. The music still pounded dully from inside, and the crowd was loud at the front of the building. Turning, he started to walk the other way and drew up short.

"Kristie, what are you doing out here?"

"Waiting for you. I know you leave this way sometimes." Kristie, a doe-eyed brunette beauty, fluttered her eyelashes up at him.

"Listen…if it's about Fintan, I can't help you with him. We're not all that close. You really need to work things out with him." Mac kept a careful distance from her. The streetlight glinted off a sheen of tears in her eyes and his heart fell. He hated seeing women cry.

"He hates me." A tear ran down her cheek.

"No, he doesn't. He hates arguing with you, I'm sure. That's two different things."

"All he does is look at other women."

"I'm sure that's not the truth. Hey, listen. You just have to talk to him." Despite himself, Mac patted her shoulder awkwardly. "It'll work out."

"I just want him to see me." A fierce note entered her voice.

"I swear to you he does."

"Maybe not, but he will now." With that, Kristie turned

and wrapped her arms around Mac's neck, and kissed him full on the mouth.

Flashbulbs exploded around them and Mac's stomach twisted in disgust.

She'd set him up – and now he was screwed.

CHAPTER 6

*N*iamh had just returned home from a work shift at the library when her phone chimed with a new text message.

I really need to talk to you. Can I come over?

Mac. Niamh's heart did a funny little flutter and she closed her eyes for a moment, debating whether it was smart to have him up to her apartment. But her instincts told her that he needed her, and she reminded herself that everyone always took from Mac – he rarely asked for help. At least from the little she'd learned about him thus far.

Sure, what time?

Niamh jumped as her apartment door buzzed. Well, now, he really needed to stop with the "just showing up" act. Hastily glancing around the apartment to see if anything incriminating was sitting out, she grabbed a lace bra off the bed, shoved her nightstand drawer closed, and took a quick glance in the mirror to make sure she wasn't a total mess. She'd already changed into loose tartan pajama pants and a soft fleece top, so there wasn't much else she could do but buzz Mac up.

"Hi," Niamh said, when she opened the door. "Sure and you were meant to get less creepy, right?"

"I texted you first this time, didn't I?" But there was no teasing note in Mac's voice, and his shoulders were hunched in his track jacket. Tension roiled from him in waves.

"Mac, what's wrong? Come in." Niamh stepped back and gestured for him to enter. Mac paused and looked around, nodding once as though he approved, and then turned to look at her. His eyes were moody in his handsome face.

"You haven't heard?"

"Heard what?" Niamh closed the door behind her and locked it, before moving across the room to put the kettle on her little stove. "Tea?"

"Please. Your place is nice."

"Thanks." Niamh laughed. "I'm sure it's a far cry from yours, but it suits me."

"It feels warm and comforting, I like it. It feels like a real home."

Niamh turned to see him just standing in the middle of her studio, a big hulk of a man, and she crossed to him.

"Tell me what I haven't heard." Niamh surprised herself when she reached out and patted his arm. "You seem upset."

"I am." Mac looked around again and when he spotted her little television, he walked over and turned it on with the remote. Flipping through the channels, he settled on a news station and pointed.

"And in a huge upset for one of our favorite rugby players, William "Mac" Macgregor was photographed making out with team captain Fintan Holister's girlfriend outside Club Eleven last night. Will the team be able to come back from this or will it fracture the ties that bind…" The newscaster read, glee in his voice. Mac snapped the television off and turned back to Niamh, his face contorted.

"It's everywhere," Mac said.

"Oh, Mac." Niamh returned to the stove and poured the hot water into mugs. "You've gone and gotten yourself into trouble now."

"I…I didn't…" Mac cut his words off and just looked at her when she brought him a mug. Niamh gestured to the little love seat, but Mac took one look at it and dropped to a pillow on the floor in front of it instead.

"Have you spoken to Fintan? What are you going to do?"

Mac just glanced up at her for a moment, and she felt something shift in the air around him…and was surprised to feel as though he was measuring her and finding her wanting. Was that disappointment that lingered in his striking blue eyes?

"He won't speak to me. In fact, nobody will. It appears I've been tried and found guilty."

"But…I mean…the photo was right there." Much to Niamh's annoyance, she added silently. The skinny brunette had been wrapped passionately around Mac and he certainly didn't seem to be fighting her off.

"Do you honestly believe…ach, never mind. Listen, I just need to get out of here for a while. Stories like this happen every once in a while, and it's good to get out of town. People move on."

"I suppose they do. There's always the next scandal," Niamh said. She blew on her tea and then took a cautious sip, trying to get a read on the mix of energy that was flowing through the studio, not to mention her own myriad emotions. Hadn't he just taken her to dinner? And two days later he's kissing another woman. Oh, that wasn't going to look good for her either, Niamh realized. "Oh, are you coming to warn me about the press? Since I was the most recent woman supposedly dating you then?"

"It's likely they'll be looking to capture your reaction as well," Mac bit out.

"So I should lay low?"

"If you don't feel like being mobbed by the press or made out to be a jealous ex-girlfriend, yeah, likely. Feck, I hate this part of fame. I really do."

Niamh's heart twisted a bit for him. Not that she approved of kissing his mate's girl, but everyone made mistakes. Having the whole world looking on while you did couldn't be all that fun. She decided to say as much.

"Listen, everyone makes mistakes. It's not easy to live under heightened scrutiny like you are. I can imagine it has to be really difficult to navigate."

"And everyone believes what they want to believe anyway…" Mac said.

"Mac…"

"Listen, your dad invited me to Grace's Cove. Do you think that offer still stands?"

"Wait, what…" Niamh's mouth dropped open. "You want to go to Grace's Cove?"

"Sure, why not? It sounds nice. Small town. Great pub, I hear. Probably not a lot of paparazzi."

"The local gossips might as well be," Niamh muttered, causing Mac to crack his first smile since he'd arrived.

"Feck it, right? I have the time coming and I can train anywhere. It will do me some good and get me out of this mess."

A mess you got yourself in, Niamh added silently.

"Mac, I don't even know if I'm going back to Grace's Cove. I only submitted my proposal this morning..." Niamh glanced at her phone as it dinged again, this time signaling an email. When she saw it was from her professor, she held up the phone. "Well, talk about timing..."

"Your professor?" Mac guessed.

"Yep. I'll just be taking a wee look here..." Niamh opened the email and scanned it before letting out a happy little cheer. "He approved it! I get to do my research!"

"That's awesome, Niamh. I'm really happy for you. When would you go?"

"Likely this weekend. The library already has someone training in my position. I'll just need to pack up my plants and few other things – I have a potential subletter lined up to take over my lease for the semester. So, in theory, I guess I can just go get started."

"I can help you pack." Mac's tone was hopeful and she sighed.

"Mac, are you trying to hide from the world?" And your actions, Niamh thought, but then tried to shove the judgmental voice away. People make mistakes, she told herself, particularly after a few drinks. She'd made a few in her early years of University.

"I am. Listen, I've got a big car. Why don't we pack your stuff up and drive down to Grace's Cove together? Unless you have a car?"

"I don't, actually." Again, Mac would be solving a problem for her and saving her father from having to make the trip to Dublin and back.

"So? Let me be your moving truck and your muscles. I carry boxes really well." Mac flexed a muscle for her and Niamh smiled.

"And then what? We're getting to Grace's Cove and you're just what…hanging at my heels all day? I've told you I've work, haven't I? Sensitive work."

"I know, I know. The famous guy can't disrupt your experiments. This may surprise you, Niamh, but I'm not entirely incompetent. I can fill my own time."

"I didn't mean to be implying you were…I just…I'm having a hard time seeing you hanging out in the village away from all the flash of city life." Niamh laughed and tucked her feet under her on the loveseat. "There's not much nightlife you know. A few decent restaurants. But it's a working man's village. Fishermen. Builders. That kind of thing."

"Sounds great. I'm in. When can we leave?"

"And…" Niamh spoke right over him, trying to stop what she felt was a train going off the tracks. "Where are you going to stay? You can't stay with me. We barely know each other."

"I bet your dad would be able to find a spot for me."

Niamh just narrowed her eyes at him, and he chuckled.

"Surely there are places to let in Grace's Cove. I looked it up, you know. It seems to be a popular tourist spot in the summer. I don't think I'll have any trouble finding a spot to sleep."

Niamh knew at least a dozen local women who would be more than helpful in that area. Pushing her annoyance aside, Niamh took a deep breath and leveled a look at Mac.

"Why do I feel like you've already made up your mind?"

"If you tell me no, I'll respect that." Mac's eyes held hers, and she could feel the truth of his words. "I just... you're my friend. I could use a friend right now."

"Alright then," Niamh smiled when lightness filled his face. "I'm not sure if you're ready for Grace's Cove or if Grace's Cove is ready for you...but, against my better judgment, you may come along. However! I do have some rules."

"Name them."

"You don't interrupt my lab-time. I'm serious about my work."

"Got it. You won't see me during your work hours."

"No sleeping with my cousins or family or anyone like that."

"The only person I want to sleep with is you." The words were out faster than he could stop them, and they hung there, suspended in the air between them.

"I..." Niamh fanned her face and laughed. "You do have a way of making women melt, don't you?"

"It's part of me charm?" Mac asked hopefully, infusing a playful note into his voice, and they moved past the moment that had threatened their fragile new friendship.

"Based on recent events and these gossips you have

mentioned, I will be a choir boy, I promise. You will not be hearing anything nefarious about me."

"Why do I get the feeling that trouble follows you whether you like it or not?"

"That's not my fault! At least not all of it. Some of that is the price of fame."

"You're not wrong there, I suppose. Well, then, let's give it a go."

"Are those my only rules? Don't bother you at work and don't sleep around?"

"Should I make more?" Niamh narrowed her eyes at him.

"Nope. I'm good with clear-cut instructions. Thank you." The last was said with deep sincerity, and warmth washed through Niamh at his words. How had this man not been able to form more friendships? He clearly needed taking care of. Had people just always been in the habit of using him? Determined to not be the person who would ever rely upon him like that, Niamh smiled.

"You know what, Mac? I think this is going to be great for you. I'm happy to have you along."

"I appreciate that."

CHAPTER 7

$\mathcal{N}$iamh had to stop herself at least a dozen times from using her telekinesis to help with her packing while Mac was there. It was a useful power to have, but she'd probably grown to rely upon it a bit too much what with living by herself for a while now. It didn't take long to sort through her things, though Niamh had to forcibly stop Mac from gleefully wanting to pack up her underwear drawer. Soon, she had a few duffle bags, her plants, and several boxes of books and lab equipment stacked up on one side of her studio. The rest of her personal items that she didn't want the subletter to use they'd put in two large plastic bins and Mac would put them in the storage locker in the basement.

"I guess that's it. Mac…it's late." Niamh yawned and checked her watch. It was close to three in the morning. The man had insisted they get started on packing immediately, even though she didn't have to rush back to Grace's Cove.

"Just trust me on this…" Mac stood by her door, car keys in hand. "I drove my truck today since the paps only know my bright orange Porsche. If we get this loaded now, we can likely avoid any press coverage."

"I…wow, sure. You're living in a whole different world than I, aren't you?" Niamh shook her head.

"Unfortunately, yes."

"And we load up…then what? Don't you need to stop at home for your stuff?"

"I have a bag in the car. I always have one packed because we travel so much."

Niamh blinked blearily at him.

"You are just ready at any moment to leave for an undetermined amount of time?"

"Yes."

"Huh. I guess no plants to water or animals to take care of?"

"No. I've always wanted a dog. But it doesn't really make sense."

"Well, you'll have loads of dogs to play with in Grace's Cove. I think every one of my family members has one." And some people I know can even speak to them… Niamh thought of Kira and her particular talent of communicating with animals.

"Grace's Cove is sounding better and better."

Niamh just looked at him for a moment before speaking. "Mac…are you sure this is what's best? Shouldn't you stay here and work things out with your teammates? Couldn't your career be on the line?"

"My career, no. I have a fairly ironclad contract. The

issues with my teammates…well, we'll see what time brings with that. This may come as a surprise to you, Niamh, but many of these men act far worse than I do. At the end of the day, we have to be rolling with the punches. Once we're on the pitch, well, that's it, then. Time to play the game."

"It just feels a bit like… I don't know. Avoiding your problems?"

"I wouldn't say avoiding. Just postponing dealing with them really. If I stick around right now the press will have a field day. It's better for everyone involved that I take off for a bit. Trust me on this one."

"If you're certain then…" Niamh looked around and sighed. She could dearly use a few hours of sleep. "I suppose we can hit the road. Even though it's the middle of the damn night."

"No bother there, Niamh. I'll drive. You have a rest." Mac picked up two of her duffle bags making them look as light as pillows and left her apartment. Niamh wasn't sure how she would feel about sleeping next to Mac in the car. She still didn't really know him all that well…it just felt like it would be too intimate.

The packing went smoothly and within the hour, Niamh and Mac were barreling down the road in his sleek black SUV. Niamh blinked drowsily at Mac in the light from the dash, wondering just how she'd ended up here of all places.

"Why don't you close your eyes for a bit? I've got the GPS set." Mac glanced at her and gave her a smile. "Don't worry, I'm a good driver. I often just go on long drives to clear my head. Listen to music. Turn off my phone and get away from it all."

Niamh wondered what it would be like to have to hop in a car and turn off the phone in order to get any peace. The more she was around Mac, the more she was learning that the pressures of celebrity were intense.

"I'm not certain I can sleep. I'm too keyed up. I haven't even messaged my parents yet."

"Time enough for that in the morning."

"Do you have favorite routes?" Niamh tried to stifle a yawn and slid deeper into the plush seat.

"Routes? For when I go on my drives?"

"Yes."

"Sure and I do like to change it up. Sometimes I'm in the mood for fast. Other times I just like a wee wander. See where things take me." Mac's voice got softer and softer and Niamh's eyes drifted closed.

When Niamh woke, she sat straight up, looking wildly around – her heart hammering in her chest.

"It's okay, you just drifted off for a while."

Niamh blinked at Mac as the fuzziness wore off from her brain.

"I...how long..." Her voice was raspy and she reached for her bottle of water. How long had she been sleeping? Did she snore? Did she...do anything else? Like make her water bottle float through the air? It was one of the reasons Niamh preferred living alone. There was no scaring off roommates or awkward explanations about situations that she couldn't really explain away. It was also why she'd never actually slept over at a man's house before.

Too much to risk.

"Most of the drive. In fact, we should be there shortly."

Niamh wiped the sleep from her eyes and looked out the window. Sure enough, the sun was already up and they were nearing the outskirts of Grace's Cove – Niamh recognized the signpost for the Bronsan's farm. Mac must have driven straight through without stopping once.

"I'm a horrible co-pilot," Niamh said. "I should have stayed up and kept you company so you didn't drift off."

"It's really not a problem at all, love. I told you I like driving. Plus, I've been too revved on adrenaline since this all happened to want to sleep anyway."

"I suppose I should be calling my parents." Niamh reached for her purse.

"Will it matter much? It looks like we're minutes away. Sure and this is a pretty spot, isn't it now?"

Niamh paused and watched as the SUV came over the top of a hill and pretty little Grace's Cove opened up below them. It was a small harbor town, with colorful houses and shops clustered on the streets surrounding the water, cocooned by large rolling green hills behind them. The sun played across the water, turning it a moody grey-blue this morning, and the fishermen's boats had long ago left the docks.

"It is at that. Ah, well, it's been a bit since I've been home. It's nice to see it." Warmth filled Niamh's heart and she realized just how much she was looking forward to spending a few months in Grace's Cove. She loved university and her studies, but she wasn't particularly fussed about city-life. Having grown up near the hills, nature still called to her more than nightclubs and bars did.

"It's this street." Niamh indicated a street just outside

the main little downtown and Mac dutifully turned the car. They followed the windy road in silence before coming across a pretty white farmhouse-style cottage. It wasn't overly grand, but it also wasn't very small. It had suited their family and though her father often suggested upgrading, Niamh's mother loved the house and so that's where they stayed.

"This is nice." Mac pulled the SUV to a stop in the small drive by the house next to two cars. Niamh saw the front curtain twitch, and took a deep breath in. She'd never brought a man home before and really had no idea how this was going to be received. She hopped quickly out of the car, and rounded the hood, but the front door was already opening.

"Niamh!" Morgan, Niamh's mother, didn't look a day over twenty in Niamh's opinion. It was annoying, really, but she hoped those genetics worked in her favor down the road. In seconds, the two women stood in the driveway hugging, rocking back and forth.

"I've missed you," Niamh said.

"And I you. You should've called. We would have had breakfast ready."

"It was a last-minute decision."

Worried eyes, twins of her own, studied her from her mother's face.

"Something's wrong."

"No, not at all. Well, not for me at least, I don't think. My proposal was approved, so I'm here for the duration. Just a touch earlier than I was expecting and all."

"And this must be the footballer." Morgan lifted her

eyes above Niamh's head. Turning, Niamh found Mac approaching her from the car.

"Yes, Mac…please meet my mother, Mrs. Kearney."

"You can call me, Morgan. Nice to meet you, Mac." Morgan held his hand for a moment longer than usual, studying his face closely. Seeming to come to a conclusion, she nodded once.

The crunch of gravel had them all turning. Niamh's father strode across the driveway, a mutinous look on his face.

"Da! It's good to see…" Niamh let out a shocked squeak as Patrick threw a neat punch directly into Mac's face. Mac stumbled back, but he did not fall. "Dad! You can't just…no!"

"Come on, Niamh." Morgan's grip on Niamh's arm was like steel. "Let's go inside."

"Mum, we can't just leave them like this…" Niamh tried to tug her arm away, but Morgan was already dragging her across the yard. "They'll kill each other."

"Patrick, darling?" Morgan pitched her voice over the grunts that were now sounding from the men who tussled in the front lawn.

"Yes, dear?"

"No murdering anyone in the yard. And stay away from my hedges. I just trimmed them."

"Of course, darling."

"I can't believe you're just letting them…" Niamh craned her neck to try to get a glimpse of what was happening as her mother shoved her inside.

"Sort things out. That's what they're doing, Niamh. We'll just leave them to it then."

"But…"

"But what? Do you think your man can't take care of himself?"

"He's not my man." Niamh sighed and pinched her nose. "He's only a friend."

"Even better then. Put the kettle on and wash your hands. I'll expect them in shortly."

CHAPTER 8

"What were you thinking with that forward pass? You could have been clean through. It was obvious to even the punters in the cheap seats that he was a mile ahead of you. If you had kept your head, you would have been between the sticks no problem, gotten your record, and the game would have wrapped up before half time. Instead, I almost get a bloody heart attack watching those last forty minutes. It's a good job Ireland won in the end or the tabloids would have had you for breakfast."

"Sure and it was a mistake on my part. It happens." Mac nodded into his cup of tea.

Niamh sat, her eyes wide, and looked between her father and Mac, who now sat at the breakfast table in the kitchen while Morgan cooked eggs at the stove. Mac's eye had already grown puffy from the punch her father had thrown, and Patrick had a good scrape across his knuckles. Two minutes ago the men had been ready to kill each other, and now they were talking about rugby of all things?

"I…" Niamh began, but Patrick interrupted her.

"If you'd keep your head in the game, you'd get your record, you understand? You'd be the top in Ireland."

"What record?" Distracted, Niamh glanced to Mac and was surprised to see a faint flush tinge his cheeks.

"Top scoring, darling. Right now, it's Ronan O'Gara. The lad has over one thousand points. Your man here is gaining on him." Patrick gestured with his cup of tea. "If he doesn't make stupid mistakes, that is."

"Da!" Niamh glared at him, flabbergasted. Leaning back, she held up a hand before either man could delve further into sports talk, none of which she understood. "Can you please explain to me why you were feeling the need to go on and have a swing at my friend here? That's not exactly the polite welcome you were promising on the phone the other day, is it now?"

"It was an honest misunderstanding. No bother on my part," Mac assured her.

"Misunderstanding? What could he possibly misunderstand? That is no way to act. Mother, I can't believe you allowed this…" Niamh looked askance at Morgan as she came to the table with her pan and dished up scrambled eggs onto the plates.

"Well, now, Niamh. Your father is a grown man. I certainly can't control what he does."

Patrick snorted, and then both men started laughing.

"Sure and you're a love, you are, Morgan. But we both know you hold the reins in this relationship."

Her mother bent and pressed a kiss to Patrick's cheek.

"And don't be forgetting it now, darling."

"Is anyone going to enlighten me on just what is going

on? And also, he just hit you! You're not mad at him?"
Niamh gestured from Mac to her father.

"Nah, as I said – honest misunderstanding. I would've
done the same."

"But…" Niamh glanced up as her mother came over
with her laptop and put it next to her plate. "What is this?"

"Have a look, Niamh. You might understand better."
Morgan squeezed Niamh's shoulder while Niamh leaned
over to read the headline on a gossip website.

Star Rugby Player breaks University Student's heart.

"Oh, please. Like anyone reads…" Niamh trailed off as
her mother began to flip through websites.

*Rugby Star Mac MacGregor has two women fighting
over him.*

*University student, Niamh Kearney, pines for the rugby
star she loves.*

*Broken hearts! Niamh Kearney embarrassed after
rugby star Mac MacGregor goes for the gold with team
captain's girlfriend.*

*The claws are out! Who will win Mac's heart – Niamh
or Kristie?*

With each headline came increasingly unflattering
photos of Niamh. Photos of her walking down the street
distracted in her thoughts. Photos of her shopping at the
market. But the main one that ran was from Bee & Bun
where she'd been furious with Mac for dumping coffee on
her laptop. Taken out of context, it looked like she was
yelling at him for something else.

Like breaking her heart.

"Oh. My. God." Niamh looked accusingly at Mac.
"They know my name! Have you seen these?"

"I don't need to see them. I knew this was coming," Mac said quietly. He reached over and squeezed her hand gently before she snatched it back.

"There's a poll on this one…" Niamh said, her horror rising along with the bile in her stomach. "Apparently, Kristie is in the lead to shag you. It seems I'm not posh enough to win a man like you over."

"Well, now, that's bollocks, isn't it?" Patrick looked offended. "You're more posh than most women I meet. Beautiful, smart, well-educated. Boy, are you saying you wouldn't want to be with my daughter?"

"Um." Mac cleared his throat, torn. Obviously he didn't want another fist in his face if he said the wrong thing.

"Please tell me you didn't just ask him if he would shag me over another woman?" Niamh's voice rose to a scary pitch as she glared at her father.

"Oh, right, right. I got caught up. What I'm saying love…is that any man should be honored to have you as a partner. Not like this Kristie girl. Let me look at her…" Patrick grabbed the laptop and scrolled the computer screen. His face went from angry to considering. "I mean, well, I can see her appeal and all."

"Patrick!" Morgan warned.

"But nothing like you, darling. Can't even hold a candle to you. Nope, not at all. Look…she's got that nasty look about her. You can see it in the eyes, right Morgan?"

Niamh leaned back and looked at the ceiling, blowing out a long breath.

"Yes, I see it. She's a mean woman." Morgan said from where she now leaned over Patrick's shoulder. "What in the world were you doing kissing her when you've got someone like Niamh?"

"Do I need to tattoo this on my forehead?" Niamh slapped her hand on the table, causing her mother to shoot her a warning look and Mac to look away as he bit back a smile. "I am not dating Mac. He is not my man. We are not together." Niamh punctuated her words with a finger in the air, pointing back and forth between her and Mac.

"That's all fine and lovely, darling, but you'll forgive us for jumping to that conclusion with the tabloids as they are and you showing up to breakfast with him at our doorstep. After being together all night," Patrick said.

Niamh thought she might scream.

"In all fairness…" Mac interrupted her melt-down. "I showed up at her doorstep and asked if I could take you up on that offer of a stay in Grace's Cove. It just happened to align with the timing of the news on her schoolwork. It was easy enough for me to be helping her to pack and just get on the road."

"I was wondering why I hadn't heard from you," Morgan said, putting the dishes in the sink. "I was going to check on you today after all the news reports."

"So you're staying a while then?" Patrick eyed Mac.

"Yes, if I'm not too much of a bother to Niamh. I have my rules."

"What are the rules?" Morgan asked.

"Wait…" Niamh interrupted.

"Don't bother her when she's working and don't, uh, date any of her friends." Mac said.

"Well, now, if you're just friends, why do you care who he dates, Niamh?" Patrick looked at her and for a brief moment she considered that maybe, just maybe, murder *should* be allowed this morning.

"Would you like to stay here?" Morgan interrupted smoothly, seeing the mutinous look on Niamh's face.

"Mother…" Niamh looked at her like she'd lost her mind.

"What? He's your friend and your father did invite him to stay, didn't he then?"

"Thank you, no. It's fine. I'll be looking to rent a spot of my own. Hopefully something with some space for training," Mac said.

"There's a pitch outside town, but it's open-air. Maybe not the best time of year for it," Patrick said, nodding to the window where the rain had begun to fall.

"Even if I have a bit of space in a living room. I can use weights. Go for runs. It'll be just fine."

"Best get you up to the pub, then. Cait will know what's currently available. I don't think I have anything in our properties."

Her father had taken an interest in real estate under Cait's husband, Shane's, tutelage. He'd picked up a few properties over the years, but they were largely meant for long-term leases now.

"I'd appreciate that then."

"I can take you over there later, or you can have a wander. It's just up the way it is." Patrick nodded to him as he stood. "I'll be seeing you for a pint later at the pub then?"

"Sure, that's grand."

"Well, now, glad that's all sorted and you have a new drinking mate. Thanks for assaulting my friend…" Niamh called down the hallway as her father left with a cheerful whistle.

"Why don't you run on with Mac and get him sorted with Cait then? I've got to get to the gallery myself," Morgan said. "Leave the dishes, I'll get to them in a bit."

"But…" Niamh wanted to get herself sorted. Hadn't Mac said he was a grown man who could take care of his own needs?

"Don't be rude to a visitor in this house, Niamh. You'll do as I say."

"Fine. I have to use the restroom first." She all but stomped from the kitchen, feeling like a moody teenager, but not before she heard Mac speak to her mother.

"I'd choose Niamh in a second, if she'd have me. I hope you know that."

"I don't doubt it, boyo. I don't doubt it."

Niamh's heart did a funny little twist in her chest, and she closed the door tightly behind her. Staring at herself in the mirror, she noticed the flush in her cheeks and that her eyes looked bright – not like someone who had only had a few hours of sleep in a car.

Oh no, she lectured herself as she found some mouthwash and swigged it around. No, no no.

You do not fall for this man. Nope, you do not. Giving herself a stern look in the mirror, as though she could intimidate her heart into listening to her thoughts, Niamh flipped the lights off and went to introduce Mac to Grace's Cove.

CHAPTER 9

"Sorry about my father. That was a bit intense, wasn't it then?" Niamh said as they trudged shoulder to shoulder, rain slickers on, down the road to Gallagher's Pub.

"I've had worse." Mac shrugged, moving to the outside of the sidewalk and nudging Niamh to the inside when a car sped past them. "It's kind of nice, actually. He's looking out for you. I can't be faulting a man for that now, can I?"

"When unnecessary violence is used, yes, you can be. How's the eye?" Niamh turned to look at him.

"Ach, it's nothing. I've had worse deciding who gets first slice of pizza after a match. Your father and I understand each other, Niamh. You're lucky to have him, that's the truth of it."

The longing in his voice reminded Niamh sharply of what Mac had told her of his upbringing and she dropped it, realizing that she might be unintentionally hurting him by chattering on about how her father had defended her honor. Mac was right. At least Patrick had stood up for her. Mac didn't seem to have a lot of people ready to do that for him.

"Mac!" A chorus of shrieks caused Niamh to draw up short and her mouth dropped open when a group of boys clad in rain jackets raced across the road to surround Mac.

"Is it really you?"

"I can't believe you're here."

"Can we play a match with you?"

"Will you teach us how to kick?"

"Da says you're the best rugby player in the world." This from a pink-cheeked boy with bright, hopeful eyes.

"I'm working on it, lad. But you could be too someday, if that's what you want." Mac patted the boy's shoulder and his eyes grew wider.

"Mac! Can you sign my ball?" One kid held out his rugby ball hopefully.

"Um," Mac patted his pockets and then looked to Niamh who just shook her head.

"To the pub. Cait will have a marker for you to use."

The boys followed Mac down the street talking about passes, kicks, and scrums...none of which Niamh really understood. But what she did understand was that Mac really cared what the kids had to say. He took his time with each one, considering their questions, and answered them all seriously. By the time they'd reached the front door of the pub, Niamh had a newfound respect for Mac and how he treated even the youngest of his fans.

"It's not open." Mac pointed to the bright doors of the pub.

"She's always open, more or less." Niamh pushed the

door open and stepped inside where warm lighting, the smell of lemon cleaner, and lilting Celtic music greeted her. "Cait? It's Niamh here. I'm just popping behind the bar for a pen."

"Niamh! Out in a bit. Go on then." A voice drifted from the back courtyard.

Gallagher's Pub was like a second home to her, Niamh thought, as she crossed the worn wooden floor to the long expanse of bar that dominated one side of the room. Ornate mirrors lined the wall behind the bar, and glass shelves showcased the high-end whiskey. Across the room, intricate wooden booths lined the walls, and smaller tables and chairs – which were often pulled to the side for dancing - dotted the main floor. Vintage Guinness posters, Celtic art, and old lanterns added charm to the space, and happiness washed through Niamh at being home.

Niamh rummaged through the drawer beneath the cash register and came out with a marker. She passed it across the bar to Mac who dutifully signed the ball, and then anything else that was handed to him by the growing crowd of children. Finally, Niamh clapped her hands together.

"That's enough. You're on to school now, aren't you then? Go on…" Niamh shooed the children and they raced outside, excitement shining in their eyes. "That was nice of you."

"They're nice kids. It's fun to talk to fans."

"Yes, but you've had no sleep, have no idea where you're staying, and the press are hounding you – you didn't have to spend the time with them. Everyone will know you're here in short order now. Don't you think the press will come this way?"

"They might. They might not." Mac smiled gently at her. "It's a lot easier to chase stories in Dublin than it is to drive across the country. Plus, I feel like your network of gossips will alert me to any reporters in the area."

"Likely true," Niamh admitted. "It's slow season, so we know pretty much anybody new who comes through."

"Niamh! Grand to see you." Cait came in from outside carrying a massive wooden pole that towered over her head. Mac immediately leapt into action and raced across the room to take it from her. "Oh, that's nice of you then. And who do we have here?"

"I'm William MacGregor. But you can call me Mac."

"Right, the rugby player. You're a good one then, aren't you?" Cait, a pint-sized tornado of energy stared up at Mac.

"I try to be."

"Well, that's all we can do, isn't it then?" Cait measured Mac for a moment, and then gave a small nod before turning to throw her arms around Niamh when Niamh crossed the room to her.

"I've missed you! I'm so glad you're here. Morgan tells me you'll be here a while?"

"Yes, 'tis true. I'm here for a few months now."

"Even better. And is Mac your…"

"Friend. A friend in need actually." They both turned and looked at where Mac continued to hold the piece of lumber.

"What are you doing out in the rain anyway?" Niamh asked, distracted.

"Mac, do you mind carrying that back out? I'll show you both what I'm thinking."

"No bother." Mac followed the ladies dutifully outside to where Cait had converted the outdoor courtyard at Gallagher's pub into a funky little sitting area with fairy lights, potted plants, and mismatched tables and chairs.

"I'm thinking I want to enclose this for winter and have heaters out here." Cait pointed along the side of the stone walls that closed in the courtyard. "It can get so warm with the bands that people might like stepping outside to cool down or have a smoke. So, I was using the pole to see how much space those warming heater towers would take up."

"Like this?" Oblivious to the rain, Mac walked around with the large piece of wood and stood with it in various areas of the courtyard.

"Yes! Exactly like that. Okay, thank you, that gives me a much better visual. If I took out a table and chairs, and moved things around a bit, there would still be space. Thoughts?"

"It's a good idea. You could do with maximizing all the space you have."

"Don't I know it? We get busier and busier every year." Cait laughed up at her and waved for Mac to come in out of the rain.

"Cup of tea for you both?" Cait bustled toward the kitchen.

"Coffee for me, if you have it," Niamh said.

"Same," Mac nodded.

"I'll be right out. Have a seat." Cait nodded to the bar and they both settled onto stools. Mac craned his neck and looked around, before knocking his knuckles against the bar.

"This is a nice place. It's got that…come in, sit down, hang out a while vibe. Where anyone is welcome, you know? No lines to get in. No VIP rooms."

"Definitely no VIP rooms." Niamh chuckled at the thought. Shifting on the stool, she crossed her feet, and smiled when Cait returned with two steaming cups of coffee.

"I added a touch of sugar and cream to both, hope that's not a bother."

"Just right. Thanks, Cait."

"Well, now, tell me what brings you here so early on?" Cait, unable to sit still, ducked behind the bar and began pulling out bottles from the rail and lining them along the top of the bar. She wiped each bottle off and then made a note in a little notebook after examining how full they were.

Niamh knew that Cait could pull it out of their heads if she wanted to know what they were doing in her pub. It was only out of politeness that Cait would restrain herself from reading other people's thoughts. But she could if she wanted to. Part of Grace O'Malley's lineage as well, Cait's powers manifested in being able to read people's minds. It certainly helped in Cait's line of work, but Niamh had to imagine it would be difficult to find peace. No wonder Cait was constantly on the move. If she kept busy she didn't have to accidently overhear unwanted thoughts.

"Mac needs a place to hide out." Niamh grinned at Cait.

"Ah, on the run from the law? Kill someone? Piss off the fae?" Cait rattled off.

"Sure and I hope I never have any dealings with the fae," Mac said, his eyes wide. Cait slid a quick glance at Niamh who shifted her eyes away. The fae were very real, that much Niamh *did* know. There were legends of them woven through Ireland and many people enjoyed recounting the stories to tourists. But there were those that still believed, or like Niamh and Cait, *knew* that the fae were real. But that was a story for another day, Niamh thought, and tuned back into the conversation.

"So it's the press you're running from. Well, sure and it's not likely we'll get many reporters through this way," Cait said. "But we'll keep an eye out for you. In the meantime, what are you needing for accommodation? What will you be doing with your time here?"

"I can help you build your courtyard," Mac surprised them both with offering.

"You're a builder as well then?" Cait eyed Mac appraisingly.

"I've dabbled here and there. But I'm smart and a hard worker. That should go a ways, right?"

"Sure, and James could use the help. Michael's gone and hit his hand with a nail gun."

"Ouch." Niamh winced. She took a sip of her coffee and studied Mac. Why in the world was he offering to help build the pub's courtyard? He certainly didn't need the money. And didn't he need to be focusing on his training? Surely this wasn't his idea of a calming vacation to get away from it all?

"Yes, it's a nasty wound. He'll heal up alright though.

Missed the tendons. Okay then, Mr. Rugby. I'll take it off your rent if that suits?"

"Perfectly. Are you my landlord then?" Mac grinned down at Cait.

"It looks that way. Don't worry…I've got a great space for you. It's a lovely house just up the hill. It's set a ways back so you have some privacy and it has a nice large yard behind it. Plenty of space and a really lovely view out over the water as it's at the top of the hill."

"Sounds perfect."

"It's a deal." Cait reached out her hand and Mac took it. Cait held it for a moment, once more studying him, before glancing quickly at Niamh with a knowing look in her eyes.

Just what is that look for? Niamh silently communicated with Cait, knowing the woman would pick up on her thoughts. Cait's lips twitched, but she said nothing.

"I'll just get the keys and have Niamh get you sorted as Shane isn't yet here to help with the pub."

After Cait had zipped away, Niamh turned to Mac and raised an eyebrow at him.

"You honestly want to build the courtyard here?"

"Sure, why not? It sounds fun. I like working with my hands. Plus, I'll meet new friends in town. It feels like a good way to get to know some people in the community."

"You could just come sit at the bar and have a pint. You'll be knowing everyone within a few days."

"Ah, but not as one of you," Mac clarified, his blue eyes smiling at her. "When I'm working on a project with people here, I become a part of the community. It's team-building 101."

Niamh's heart twisted when she realized just how long Mac had been using these tactics to build little family environments for himself.

Grace's Cove had brought healing to many people through the years; maybe Mac would find some of that here as well.

CHAPTER 10

*A*fter Mac had unloaded his SUV of Niamh's stuff, he'd brushed off her offer to help him settle into the rental house. At this point, he just needed a moment of space from her. Not only was he exhausted from pulling an all-nighter, but the longer he was around Niamh, the harder he was finding it to resist reaching out to touch her. He wanted to wrap a lock of her auburn hair around his finger, tug her close, and taste her lips. Instead, he had to push those feelings aside and remind himself that she had very neatly friend-zoned him.

Which was fine, really. At least that's what he told himself as he grabbed his duffle bag from the SUV and walked to his rental unit. His life was messy right now and it didn't really make sense to try and fit a relationship in. At least not one that mattered, because he'd just end up disappointing his partner. It was better if Mac just continued on with bachelorhood until he could actually devote time to maintaining a relationship. A woman like

Niamh deserved someone who could give her that level of care.

The rental house was exactly what Cait had promised it would be. It was a nice-sized cottage set back from the street with a hedge surrounding the front yard. Green hills rose behind the cottage, and large picture windows spanned the front, giving a brilliant view of the village and the harbor below. Mac was pleased to find high ceilings, an actual king-sized bed, and a generous-sized bathroom in the cottage. Oftentimes, he felt like his body wasn't built for tiny European bathrooms or beds, and it was nice to feel like he could stretch out in his space. As soon as Mac put his clothes away, he moved the furniture around in the living room so that he could clear some open floor space. Next, he returned to his SUV and unloaded the spare set of free-weights and kettlebells he kept in his car. Rolling out a few mats to cover the rug, Mac immediately stretched and began a few sets of kettlebell swings. He knew his energy was low today, but habit was habit, and he didn't want to go soft during this break time. His team counted on him, and Mac wouldn't let them down.

Even if Kristie was set on causing a rift.

Stupid woman. Mac grunted as he switched positions and began a one-armed overhead press with a weight. A jealous and nasty woman, Mac amended. She was so convinced that Fintan was interested in other women that she couldn't see that the man was half-blind for her. Something which Mac hoped Fintan would snap out of. Kristie was the type of woman that would only bring him down unless they could figure out their communication issues. If she didn't trust him, Fintan would never make her happy, and it would be a vicious cycle. One which could affect the whole team if Fintan wasn't careful.

Mac had found his team captain immediately after Kristie had kissed him. He hadn't waited for the story to break, and he certainly didn't care what Kristie thought. Instead of turning and leaving the club, Mac had stormed back inside, leaving Kristie crying in the alley with the paparazzi, and had found Fintan. The conversation hadn't gone well, likely because Fintan was in his cups, but Mac could at least content himself with doing the right thing and telling his team captain face-to-face. Once his duty was done, and Fintan had told him to bugger off, Mac had left.

At this point, Mac knew that Fintan and Kristie had to figure it out on their own. It didn't matter what the press said or did – they always crafted their own story anyway.

But what really made him angry about the whole thing was that Niamh had immediately believed that he would kiss his team captain's girlfriend.

Mac grunted again as he switched arms and went into more reps. Not only had Niamh thought he'd do something like that, but then she'd immediately forgiven him and had told him that people make mistakes. It would be easier to be angry with her for thinking the worst of him if she hadn't forgiven him right away. It was this dichotomy with Niamh that was messing with his head. It was as though he wanted her to see him in the best light, but then she went and accepted him anyway, even if he did make mistakes. It was as though his flaws were a bonus for Niamh? That couldn't be right.

Mac switched to deadlifts. Grabbing a heavier kettlebell, he added another round of reps. His whole life he'd had to hide who he was. Over and over, it had been drilled into him to work harder, be perfect, and to never show weakness.

Never show who he was.

An image of his father's face, contorted in disdain, turning his back on Mac flashed to Mac's mind. It didn't matter which time it was. There had been so many times that Mac had eventually lost count. It wasn't until his father had finally given up on him around the age of ten and he'd been left to largely fend for himself had Mac been able to breathe a sigh of relief. No attention at all was better than the constant disappointment. At that time, his father had channeled his interest into the bookies, and the focus had shifted from Mac so long as he made himself quiet and didn't cause much fuss. Mac had learned to cook for himself, do laundry, and clean up after himself. He'd done his studies without any prompting from anyone and had never missed a rugby practice.

The rugby club had been the one thing that had saved him. There, he could be a different person. At the club he wasn't the quiet boy looking for family or trying to hide who he was. No, there he could just be a boy. Making jokes with the other lads, trying out new plays, and tossing the ball around. It had also been the one area where his father had actually shown up for him. When his father remembered, he'd come to matches or periodically he'd bring home a new rugby ball for Mac. It was almost always an afterthought, but Mac had sucked up those crumbs of affection as though he was starving.

His lack of parental attendance at the matches hadn't

gone unnoticed by the other parents of the rugby club. Somehow or another, his uniforms always got mended, he'd had enough food to eat, and more than once a Christmas gift with new shoes had appeared. Mac didn't like when that happened, because even though his father allowed him to keep the gifts, he'd pay the price for it.

He always did.

Rugby had saved him. It really had. And now, in this time of trouble, Mac didn't want to let his teammates down. He would train, harder than ever, and make sure to show up on the pitch in shape and ready to play. His mates on the team knew the score – he'd been sure to tell them what had actually happened. Most of them knew Kristie and expected such shenanigans from her, so Mac wasn't worried on that front. He just had to ride this out, keep strong, and he'd be back to running plays with his mates soon enough.

Home was on the pitch and the only thing that had ever really resonated with him.

Which was why, now that he'd played for a few years and had carefully saved and invested his money, he wanted to do something meaningful to give back. How many other lonely kids out there needed a place to go? To blow off steam? To find community? Mac was well aware that a career in rugby was fleeting. Growing up the way he had, Mac knew that at any moment everything could be taken from him. Which was why he was careful with his money, despite a few splurges here and there, and it was also why he'd finally started working on his secret project.

Mac wanted to open a non-profit rugby club for children in need. Kids like him who didn't have the money for gear, or the guidance at home to help. He wanted it to be more than just a rugby club, though. He wanted a staff on hand – social workers that could help guide the kids, listen to their problems, and help them on their way. Tutors to help with problems at school. It was his dream to create the support network, community, and help he'd never had growing up. It couldn't replace parental love, that much Mac knew, but if he could save a few kids along the way, he'd feel like he'd actually made a difference with his time here.

It wasn't easy feeling like you were all alone.

Mac automatically shot his hand out a good three seconds before the vase he bumped fell to the floor. He caught it neatly mid-air and put it back on the shelf, his heart pounding as he stared at the cheerful blue hand-blown vase.

Nobody liked being the odd one out.

CHAPTER 11

*A*fter a much-needed nap, Niamh spent the afternoon settling herself back into her childhood bedroom before she tackled the project she was most excited about – setting up her lab. Her parents had given her use of the garden shed in the back and her father had even spent some time cleaning it out and upgrading a few things once he'd heard Niamh would be coming home. It was really sweet of him, Niamh thought as she stood in the doorway to the shed. Never once had her parents tried to step on her dreams or direct her to another route. Instead, they'd allowed her to make her own path, and she always knew that she had their support.

Unlike Mac.

Niamh's thoughts strayed to him as she lugged her boxes into the shed and put them on the long wooden worktable set up in the corner. His presence in her life just felt…almost overwhelming. Two weeks ago, she'd barely heard of this man, and now he'd helped her pack her apartment and had moved with her to Grace's Cove. All of it felt a little surreal and Niamh wasn't sure how she felt about the fact that her mind often drifted to thoughts of him. Already, Niamh found herself wanting to take care of Mac.

She'd always been this way – completely open-hearted. Niamh sighed as she slit the tape open on a box and began to dig through her books. Maybe because she had never felt readily accepted, aside from her family and a few friends in Grace's Cove, she'd always made an effort for others. She'd been the girl to always try and befriend a shy kid at school, or take in stray cats, or to help a wounded bird. Niamh was a fixer, and she hated seeing wounded…anything, really. Now, learning more about Mac and his vulnerable past, Niamh found herself wanting to take care of him and show him that not everyone cared only about Mac's celebrity.

"This way lies danger…" Niamh said out loud in her best movie theater narrator voice.

"Which way lies danger?"

Niamh jumped and held a hand to her pounding heart before glaring at her mother.

"You scared me!"

"Sorry, the door was open. Next time should I shout across the yard?" Morgan held two cups of tea in her hand and Niamh waved her in.

"I'm sorry. I was just lost in thoughts. And apparently talking to myself."

"I've brought you tea and I've come to supervise. Which means I'm not lifting any boxes."

"Thank you." Niamh accepted the cup gratefully and took a sip. The moody grey sky had unleashed the rain it had been holding all afternoon, so Niamh closed the shed door and flipped on the little space heater her father had thoughtfully provided. Pulling a candle from one of her boxes, she set it next to a little aloe plant and lit the wick. Soon, the scent of lavender filled the room and Niamh began to relax in the cozy space. "This is nice...what you've done here. Thank you for cleaning this out for me."

Morgan looked around from where she'd taken a seat at a little bistro-style table with two chairs set in the corner. What had once been a musty garden shed that had just been collecting tools and other miscellaneous items that had long outlived their use was now a functioning work-space. Her parents had cleaned off the shelves, added new lighting, put in a worktable, a spot to have tea, and had even thrown a brightly patterned rug down over the worn wood planks. Morgan, being Morgan, had tacked up some lovely prints of Kira's photographs of Grace's Cove on the walls, and strung a strand of twinkle lights around the ceiling to add some ambience. As labs went, it was prob-ably the most charming space that Niamh had used.

"It was a nice project to tackle. Your father has most of his tools in the garage anyway, and this space was just collecting useless things. Neither of us are much for gardening as it is. I'm glad to see it being used. In fact, once you're done with it, I may convert it into a little art space for myself."

"You're making art now? What are you into these days?" Niamh smiled at Morgan and continued to unpack her boxes.

"I'm thinking I'd like candle-making, to be honest with you. I love all the scents and pretty packaging we sell at the gallery. But Gracie says she can't keep up with demand and wants to focus really on her creams and tonics. The candles were always just a side-gig for her."

"How's she doing then? I need to go on up and see her and Kira."

"Aye, sure and they're both doing grand. They'd love to see you. Everyone would, but you've time for that now, don't you?"

"Sure, and I'm in no rush to be off for a while. It's nice being home." Niamh took a deep breath in and let it out. "It just smells different here, you know? Like earth and air and…"

"Dirt? That's the shed, darling." Morgan laughed.

"I know. But it's something you miss living in the city. It's quieter. Less chaotic. I feel more grounded here, I suppose."

"Well, you're welcome to stay as long as you like. Or as long as Mac needs." Morgan gave Niamh a knowing look over her tea.

"Ah, well then. I can't imagine he'll be staying long now, will he? He's got a team to go back to. He can't be running away forever."

"Maybe he's running to something," Morgan said, and Niamh wondered how her mother could see so clearly.

"Is that what you're thinking? You may have the right of it." Niamh shrugged one shoulder and opened another box. "He's a nice man. Nicer than I had originally thought he would be, based on what I'd read in the papers. Honestly, Mum? I think he's pretty lonely. Everyone wants something from him. But I'm not sure many people see him."

"Ah." Morgan said nothing after that, and the silence drew out until Niamh turned and looked at her.

"What does that mean?"

"Nothing, love. Nothing at all."

"You're annoying me." Niamh glared at her.

"You're a smart girl, Niamh. I'm not going to offer any opinion yet. I barely know the lad. Give it time, and we'll see what we see."

"I guess that's all we can do, really." Niamh sighed and looked at her piles on the worktable.

"What do you hope to accomplish here?" Morgan asked.

"I guess I just want to show him that people can like him for who he is. And that it doesn't need to be about what he can do for people."

"Um…" Morgan drew the word out with a small laugh. "I was meaning with your lab. Like *here*. Your studies."

"Oh!" Niamh felt the flush rush up her cheeks. Damn it, she'd just given away some of her feelings.

"I'll just tuck that bit away, shall I?" Morgan smiled into her teacup. "Give it time darling. Give it time. Grace's Cove has a way of working her magick on most people. Including yourself."

"Right, well, in regard to what I'm working on…" Niamh said pointedly, refusing to discuss anything more deeply about Mac lest she do something foolish like run up the hill and jump the poor man. "I'm hoping to be able to measure, in some manner, the energy around some of the parapsychological powers we can do."

"You want to measure magick." Morgan raised an eyebrow at her.

"I just want to see if there is a way that I can, in terms that the science world can understand, measure the energy or model of energy that happens when magick is done. Perhaps if there was a way to measure it, people could be taught to replicate it."

"Why do you think people need to be taught to replicate it?" Morgan asked.

"I don't, necessarily. But it might dispel the whole bad reputation that people with powers have. If it could be accepted more in the scientific community, then maybe children growing up with these powers wouldn't be ostracized."

"Ah, my poor girl. I hoped to shield you from what I went through." Morgan's eyes held a world of pain.

"Oh, Mum, but you did. I didn't experience even close to what you did. But your story sits with me." Niamh held a hand to her heart. "It sits with me here. It is a part of me and the threads of my life. There are other children out there experiencing that pain. We can help them."

"Well, I'm not sure if this is the best route to helping them or not, but I can say that I've always appreciated your brilliant mind. You'll find a way to help, no matter what. I'm so very proud of you." With that, Morgan stood and picked up her empty teacup. Pressing a kiss to Niamh's cheek, she moved to the door.

"Don't work too long. We've got a dinner guest."

"Wait, what…who?"

"Mac, of course. You can't let the man eat alone his first night in Grace's Cove."

"Mum! No. Why did you invite him?" Niamh needed a little space from Mac to get her thoughts straight.

"Because that's what you do when your daughter brings a friend home. He'll be along shortly now. You might want to change."

Niamh looked down to her faded leggings and old sweatshirt and sighed. So much for finishing up her unpacking. Already Mac was interrupting her schedule. Annoyed, she blew out the candle and closed the shed door securely, following her mother through the rain to the main house.

If her heart picked up in excitement at the thought of seeing Mac again, she ignored it. Nope, it was most definitely the siren's call of a homecooked meal that was causing this excitement and that was that.

CHAPTER 12

*N*iamh didn't put any extra effort into her look for dinner that night…no she most certainly did not. She pulled on jeans, a heather green jumper, and slipped on her hoop earrings. Niamh didn't even bother with makeup, because, well, she was having dinner at her own house. This is how she dressed for family dinners. If Mac didn't think she was fancy enough, well, that was just fine. She wasn't meant to care what he thought anyway, right?

Now she was annoying even herself, so Niamh went to help Morgan in the kitchen. Her mother hummed along with the Rolling Stones playing in the background while she chopped vegetables for a salad.

"Anything I can help with?"

"I don't think so. I've just done a simple casserole and some garlic bread. It's pissing rain out and it feels like a comfortable meal for a cold night."

"It smells divine. Can I open a bottle of wine then?"

"Of course, I pulled out a new red that I like." Morgan

nodded to where the bottle of wine sat on the counter. Niamh found the opener, poured them both a glass, before settling at the little breakfast table in the kitchen. They would eat in the dining room when Mac arrived, but Niamh always enjoyed this cozy spot. She'd spent countless hours here while her parents cooked, and she worked on her homework. The wave of familiar, the love that wound through the years, washed over her and eased some of the tension in her shoulders. She'd made the right choice coming back here, Niamh decided. She'd be able to work in a supportive environment and even discuss her experiments with her family each night. If she'd stayed in Dublin she would have been conducting her experiments alone with nobody to discuss the elements of her studies with except for her professor. No, this had been the right choice. Particularly if she could manage to rope Kira or Gracie into letting her run some tests on them.

A knock sounded at the door, startling Niamh from her thoughts, and Morgan gestured with the knife to go answer.

"Hi." Niamh said, holding the door open for a dripping Mac. Had the man never heard of an umbrella? Surely there had to be one stocked in the rental house.

"Hi." Mac grinned at her and held out a bouquet of flowers and a bottle of whiskey. "This is for your parents."

"That's nice of you, isn't it? Well, go on, shake yourself off in the foyer. There's a hook for your coat." Niamh gestured to the coat rack and stuck her nose in the flowers. For a brief moment she wished that the flowers were for her, but then pushed the thought away as she waved him back with her to the kitchen. The man looked good tonight,

Niamh thought, keeping her eyes on the flowers so she wouldn't simper all over Mac. He wore fitted grey pants, a navy-blue sweater that made his eyes pop, and his hair was still damp from his shower. Or the rain. Either way, he was drool-worthy and Niamh wasn't in the mood to drool for anything other than the delicious food her mother was cooking.

"Welcome, Mac. Oh, well, now…aren't these sweet?" Morgan leaned over to sniff the flowers and nodded to Niamh to get a vase. "Thank you, Mac. Can we get you something to drink?"

"Tea would be grand."

"I'll bring it out. Niamh, why don't you take Mac to the living room after you get those flowers in some water? Your father should be along any minute now and food is almost ready. I hope you're hungry, Mac."

"Absolutely famished. I haven't had a chance to get to the grocery store yet."

Niamh wondered what he'd been doing all day then. Likely sleeping, she reminded herself. He had driven her through the night to get home.

"I like your parents' place. It's got a good feel to it," Mac said as they entered the living room.

"Yes, my mother has a good eye for art. I think she's done well with the decorating here."

Instead of a room cluttered with family photos and mementos, the living room showcased a comfortable leather sofa, a tartan armchair, and the main wall held one large painting by Aislinn. The painting depicted the sun setting over the water and the colors were vibrant and alive. A few built-in shelves surrounded the television and they held a small collection of family portraits. Mac stopped in front of one and picked it up, a grin on his face.

"That's a stubborn look if I've ever seen it."

"Oh, well, yes." Niamh crossed the room and studied ten-year-old her, surrounded by books, annoyance in her eyes at being interrupted. "I liked my time with my books, I'll admit. They had to drag me outside to play half the time."

"Not me. They couldn't get me off the pitch. It was the only place…" Mac cut off his words and Niamh looked at him, a question in her eyes.

"Dinner's ready sooner than I expected. Shall we go to the dining room?" Morgan interrupted Niamh's question. Patrick came in and gave Mac a complicated handshake, along with a couple slaps on the back. Niamh still didn't understand how they were pummeling each other in the front garden this morning and now were acting like they were doing a secret handshake to get into a club or something.

"Men are weird." Niamh took a sip of her wine and looked across the table at Mac. His presence seemed to loom over everyone else. Even with her father being a fairly fit man, Mac was just all muscle and took up a lot of space. It was enough to make anyone feel small in his proximity, and Niamh's stomach did a jittery dive thinking about Mac sweeping her up in his arms and then…

"How so?" Morgan asked, passing her the casserole dish.

"Um…" Niamh shook her head to clear her thoughts. "Just that they can fight and then be best friends. That would never fly with women. We'd be mad for weeks…"

"That's the truth of it. I can't say that men are more efficient with arguments though. Sometimes those fights never get resolved, you know? They never talk about it, and it festers for ages. Then they see each other at the pub one night and it all comes out. Tears or fists." Morgan passed the breadbasket to Niamh. "Go on then, Mac. Eat as much as you'd like. You're a growing man."

"I think he's grown, Mother." Niamh blushed.

"Thank you, Mrs. Kearney. I can't remember the last time I've had a homecooked meal." Mac dished up a healthy serving.

"Is that right? Well, I'll let you know what nights I'm cooking. You'll want to stay away the nights this one's the chef." Morgan nodded to Patrick who pretended to be wounded.

"Hey now. I'm excellent on the grill."

"Sure and that's the one thing he can do." Morgan laughed.

"We all have our strengths," Niamh said.

"So…about that last match," Patrick began.

"Nope." Morgan interrupted him. "The man clearly has to talk about rugby every day of his life. Give the lad a break, would you?"

"It's fine, really," Mac said, his eyes lighting on Niamh's, and warming her with the humor she saw there.

"You've never been to Grace's Cove?" Patrick changed the subject smoothly. He took a bite of the casserole and gave a little sound of pleasure.

"No, I haven't. From what I can see, it's a brilliant spot. I'm surprised I haven't been this way, actually."

"Well, it's a bit off the beaten path, but we like it that

way, don't we? I'm sure Niamh has given you the standard warning about the cove? If you've a mind to be wandering about?" Morgan asked.

"Um…" Mac looked at Niamh in confusion.

"No, I haven't really had the chance, what with the whole leave under the cover of darkness thing we did. Okay, so here's the deal – don't go in the cove. Simple." Niamh shrugged when her parents just stared at her. "What? That's the easiest way to keep people from harm."

"Why would I be harmed in the cove?" Mac's gaze bounced between the three of them, and Niamh wondered if he was trying to decide if they were having him on or they were just simply crazy.

"Do you want the real story or the one that we tell the tourists to keep them safe?"

"Both," Mac said.

"I like him," Morgan said. "The story we tell the tourists is to not go into the cove because of strong winds, a narrow cliff path, dangerous riptides in the water. Basically, we try to make it as unwelcoming as possible so that people will just enjoy the sight from the cliff's edge. We've even put a little locked gate at the top now so as to discourage fools from clambering down the path to the beach below."

"Sounds sensible. And the unofficial version?"

"The cove's enchanted," Niamh said, her eyes holding Mac's to see how he would respond. Where she was expecting disbelief or laughter, she instead saw understanding.

Well, now, isn't that interesting…

"Is that right?" Mac asked, taking another bite of the

casserole.

"Most people will say we're crazy. But…those who know, well, they know." Morgan shrugged.

Mac glanced to Patrick who nodded solemnly.

"When you've lived here your whole life, there's just some things you come to accept. This is one of them."

"And what happens if you step into this enchanted cove?" Mac asked.

"Ah, well, she'll toss you right back out on your bum. With many of your bones broken. I don't recommend you go there," Niamh said.

"Well, that explains why you're studying what you are," Mac said, and Niamh swallowed as her parents stilled. She hadn't told them that Mac didn't know about her, or any of her family, and now she silently warned them not to say anything to give her away.

"Of course," Niamh said quickly, "growing up around something of that nature makes you want to question the unknown more deeply. It's fascinating, really."

"Do you believe in things like that?" Morgan turned her head to Mac. "Parapsychology. Psychometry. Extra-sensory abilities? Those kinds of things?"

"I do, actually," Mac said. His response just about blew Niamh away and she gaped at him.

"Do you really?"

"Sure and why not then? I'm Irish, aren't I? We're always on about the fae and what not. There's something to be said there. But I guess I'm not sure I'm really under-standing the line between magick and extra-sensory abili-ties. Like, if you can read someone's mind or predict the future – is that magick? Or is that an extra-sensory ability?" Mac raised his eyebrows in question as he thought about it. He ripped a piece of bread in two and dabbed one side in the sauce of the casserole before chewing thoughtfully.

"I...well, I suppose it can be both, right?" Niamh said, picking her way carefully through the conversation. "Perhaps some abilities are given with magick and others might be the result of a highly-developed area of the brain."

"Ah, interesting. So like, if we all had super large prefrontal cortexes or whatever, we might be able to move things with our mind or predict the future?"

"Something like that..." Niamh's mouth had gone dry and she didn't dare look at her mother.

"Well, it's fascinating, I'll say that much. I hope you'll tell me more about your studies this summer, Niamh. I can see why the subject matter can pull a body in. I'm truly interested. Do you test everyone? How do you establish who has ability and who doesn't?" Mac asked.

"Um, yes. I'll have a control group set up," Niamh said. "Why, did you want to be in the control group?"

"I might. Unless you think I might have powers?" They all laughed at Mac's joke, but Niamh caught a flash in his eyes. There was something more there...but soon her father distracted her with a funny story about the lads trying to capture a sheep that had broken into the back door of the bakery. Soon, they were all laughing and the moment had passed leaving Niamh to wonder how this man seemed to fit so seamlessly into her life.

It was enough to make her need another glass of wine, that was for sure.

CHAPTER 13

"Go on…walk off that dinner. The rain's finally let up." Morgan waved her hands at Niamh and Mac to shoo them from her dining room. "Your father will help with the washing up."

"But Mum…Mac probably has something else to do." Niamh gave her mother a look warning her to knock it off.

"Actually, a walk sounds nice. I like walking at night in new places. It gives a different impression." Mac smiled at Niamh when she just blinked at him across the table. "You don't have to go for a walk if you don't want to."

Now Niamh would look rude if she said no, but at the same time she wanted to finish unpacking her boxes and start setting up her lab.

"You did say that you came to Grace's Cove early, Niamh. You'll have plenty of time to get your studies done, won't you?" Patrick looked at her, his eyes warm with love, before turning to confide in Mac. "She was always like this as a child, too. I had to drag her from her books most days and boot her outside."

"Most parents would be proud of their children for reading so much," Niamh grumbled as she stood. "But instead I was punished."

"I certainly don't think making you get some fresh air and stretch your legs on occasion is a harsh punishment," Morgan laughed. "Weren't you just saying how much you like being out of the city and back in nature?"

"Well, now you're making me sound like a nutter," Niamh grumbled.

"I get it. There is something about being surrounded by wide-open spaces even if you aren't always outside in those wide-open spaces." Mac grinned at Niamh, neatly rescuing her.

"Let's go for a walk then." Niamh stood. "I can see my father is working himself around to ask you more about rugby."

"Oh, right, rugby." Morgan winced. "I have no idea why I keep calling it football."

"Because your head is in the art world not the sports world." Patrick dropped a kiss on Morgan's head as he began to clear the table. "And that is perfectly fine. I mean…slightly insulting to one of the top athletes in Ireland who is sitting at your table. But just fine, none-theless."

"Sure and didn't I just feed this top athlete a nice dinner? It's not like I booted him out the door, spit on his head, and declared that I only feed footballers, now did I?" Morgan narrowed her eyes at Patrick.

"That's our cue to leave." Niamh motioned for Mac to follow her quickly as her parents began to argue, though Niamh knew it was only playful banter. She'd been lucky to have parents that rarely had huge arguments. Niamh wasn't sure her sensitive emotions could have handled being around that level of discord regularly. She just absorbed too much of the energy of the world around her.

"Well, the rain's stopped for now, but there's still a bite to the wind," Mac said as he held the door open for her. Considering his words, she grabbed a wool coat and scarf of her mother's and bundled herself inside. Moments later, they strolled in the soft light of the moon, the rain clouds having moved on for the moment. Soon, they reached the main streets of the village, and Niamh burrowed more deeply into her coat as another sharp burst of wind raced down from the hills. Light from the restaurants and homes that clustered the streets reflected softly in the puddles, and a riff of music along with laughter could be heard when the door to Gallagher's Pub opened briefly.

"What do you say? Would you like to stop in for a pint?" Mac asked, nodding to the pub.

"Um," Niamh thought about all of the people she would have to talk to, not to mention the crowd that would surround Mac, and decided against it. "I think not tonight. I'm still quite tired and if we go in there I'll have to say hello to the entire town and then it will be two in the morning before I even know it."

"Another night, then?" Mac asked and Niamh turned to look at him as he steered her gently away from the pub and down toward the water.

"Another night will be nice," Niamh said lightly. She wasn't sure that he was asking her as a date or as friends, but she figured they'd moved past the dating point by now. "Gallagher's Pub is really the heart of this town. Cait has her finger on the pulse of everything that's going on, and more often than not, most people will wander in at some point during the day. You'll meet a lot of people when you're helping with the construction there. I hope you're ready for it…because if you came here for privacy, well, it's likely not going to happen."

"I don't mind." They reached the water and began to walk along the low stone wall that hugged the harbor. "When it's just friendly interest and people wanting to meet me? Yeah, that's no bother. It's when I feel like I'm being used for something that gets my back up a bit."

"I don't blame you," Niamh said softly, pausing for a moment to lean over the stone wall and look out into the water. "It has to get tiring, I suppose, always trying to sort out people's intentions. I suspect it's probably hard for you to trust anyone, isn't it then?"

Mac leaned over the wall with her, his arm touching hers, and Niamh could swear she felt the warmth through her coat. Being near him had the weird effect of being both calming and exciting at the same time. It was like adding hot pepper to cocoa and Niamh wasn't sure if she liked it or not.

"Maybe that's my fatal flaw," Mac said after a moment of silence. "I want to believe the good in everyone. I guess…I guess I'll always be searching. That little kid who wants to believe the world will be kind to him. That someone will come along and tell him everything will be okay. That he's safe. Ach…"

Niamh's heart twisted as Mac abruptly stopped talking and rolled his shoulders back, looking away from her.

"It's not a bad trait to have, Mac." Niamh nudged his

shoulder with hers, causing him to look down at her. "So many people only see the worst. They feed off negativity. They look for what can go wrong instead of what could go right. They assume that everyone operates with ill intentions when maybe that person was just having a bad day and lashed out. There are a lot of wounded people walking around."

You're not alone, Niamh added silently. Oh, but she wanted to care for him – to show him that people could love him just for who he is. Goosebumps ran down the back of her neck at the idea of love. Where in the world did that idea come from? Love? She barely knew the man. Her own issues were popping up – this need to mother, to care for others – and she definitely needed to get that urge under control. Mac was his own man, and he certainly didn't need her hovering over him trying to heal him. Perhaps it was her classes at school that were making her think like this, Niamh decided. She'd had to take loads of psychology courses along with her science classes as she worked toward her degree. The path she wanted to take in life demanded both schools of thought, so that is what had to be happening here, as she heard the wounded notes of a lonely and lost little boy come through Mac's voice.

"I guess. It's just a trait that gets me in trouble at times. I'm always hopeful that I'm not going to get screwed… and sometimes I don't. Sometimes I do. But that's life right? Just gotta roll with it." Mac looked back out over the water.

"I hope you don't lose that," Niamh said softly, leaning into him more as the wind picked up. Automatically, Mac put his arm around her and pulled her close, rubbing his hand down her back for warmth. "I hope your fame doesn't make you jaded and burn the part of you that wants to believe the good in people. We need more people like you in the world, Mac."

Mac's arm tightened around her waist, squeezing her once as though to acknowledge her words, but he said nothing. For a moment, they stood there, huddled together against the sharp bite of the wind that whipped down the hills and across the dark water. The mood shifted…from comfort to something more…and Niamh felt nerves dance through her stomach as Mac dipped his chin to look down at her.

"I don't think anyone really sees me. Ever. But…I think you do. You just might see me, Niamh." Mac's voice was nothing but a whisper as he drew his lips close to hers, hovering achingly near, and time slowed for Niamh.

Oh, she wanted this, she realized. She really wanted this. He'd already invaded her thoughts and it was undeniable there was a chemistry between them. Making a choice, Niamh leaned in slightly, and Mac's lips brushed hers.

Instantly, heat rushed through Niamh, like throwing lighter fluid on a fire. It shocked her, the intensity of her response to the softest of kisses.

"Hey! It's Mac!"

Niamh pulled back from the kiss, stepping quickly away from Mac and turning her head to see a group of teenagers with their phones out. Immediately, she was reminded that there were no private moments with a celebrity. Mentally kicking herself for letting her guard down, Niamh reminded herself that this was not the life she wanted.

"Hey guys," Mac said. After a quick glance at Niamh, he pasted a smile on his face.

"Can we get a picture with you?" A child, wearing nothing but a track suit in the cold, asked eagerly.

"Sure, no problem."

Niamh raised an eyebrow as the kid handed her his phone, neatly cutting her from the photo, and went to stand next to Mac. Not that Niamh wanted to be in the photo, she reminded herself, and waved everyone forward to form a group around Mac.

"Be sure to get the flash on!"

"No problem," Niamh smiled through her annoyance, her emotions on a roller coaster, as she took several shots of Mac with the kids and waited while he answered questions and signed autographs. Finally, Mac stepped back from the group.

"That's all I have time for now. The lady is getting cold." With that, the kids ran off, and Niamh knew then that their private time in Grace's Cove was already over. "I'm sorry about that."

"Don't be. You can't help what other people do." Niamh shrugged one shoulder and turned to walk back toward her house. "But you do realize that those photos will be on social media already and the paparazzi can find you if they want to now?"

"It would happen anywhere that I went. My only hope is that there is something more exciting to keep them in Dublin and away from me."

"And if they follow you here? Then what?"

"Then I'll deal with it when it happens. For now, I have an early wake-up call to get to work on the courtyard."

"You're really doing it then? You're going to show up that early and be a builder?" Niamh asked as they walked up the sharp hill to her house.

"Of course. I said I would, didn't I?"

"Sure and you did. I was just wondering. Listen…" Niamh needed to address the kiss. The moment when everything stopped and she would have jumped through fire for just another second with this man. If she let it, her emotions would consume her so she needed to start compartmentalizing. As in now.

"Don't say it, Niamh." Mac stopped and grabbed her arm, turning Niamh to meet his eyes.

"But…" Niamh licked her lips, wanting another kiss from him already.

"You've already told me that this isn't the life you want. You were very clear. And, of course, the first time I kiss you it's ruined by my life choices slapping us in the face. I get it. I do. But…just don't say it. I just need to have one perfect moment that isn't ruined, or overly discussed, or splashed through the media. Can I just have that?"

One perfect moment, Niamh's heart grabbed onto those words. Nodding, she turned and continued to walk.

"The bakery on the corner there is the only one open early in the morning if you're needing a bite before your job tomorrow…" Niamh said, pointing at the small building, and Mac's sigh of relief eased the tension knotting her shoulders.

CHAPTER 14

*L*uckily for Niamh, Mac kept himself busy over the next few days as she set up her lab and began to get started with her experiments. Sure, he checked in periodically with a text message or sent her a funny picture of him on the construction site, but otherwise she'd been left largely alone. Which was exactly what she had requested of him, Niamh reminded herself for the hundredth time that day when her thoughts strayed to Mac. He was following the rules of not interfering with her work.

Work, right. Niamh shook her head and sat back in the bistro chair in her lab. She'd had a productive few days of setting up certain parameters for her study and today she wanted to just test out some of the equipment. First up, she wanted to see if she could track any sort of discernable energy patterns when she moved something with her mind.

Niamh had been stuck on how to do this particular part of the experiment for a while. To protect the privacy of, well, herself, and the other subjects, she needed to figure out a way to film the actual act happening without showing the person in the video. Niamh had put together a simple camera set up in the corner where the object to be moved was filmed on a white drop cloth. That way the person could be standing outside the video. Niamh was debating whether to show a portion of the person's body, so the video recorded them being in the vicinity or even going so far as having the person entirely in the frame, but just blurred out. For now, she wasn't trying to prove whether something like telekinesis was real. Instead, she was looking to see if the energy could be measured.

Because that's all it was, at least as far as Niamh was concerned. Universal energy. Some would call it magick. Some would call it science. Either way, it was energy. And where there was energy, there should also be a way to measure it. The real issue she was already running into was what type of energy specifically would it create? Electrical? Heat? Kinetic? She'd already begun to wonder if she'd bitten off more than she could chew.

Niamh jumped when her phone alarm sounded. Long ago, she'd learned to set alarms if she had to be anywhere, otherwise she'd get too sucked into whatever she was reading about. Now, she wrinkled her nose and sighed before reaching to turn the alarm off. Gracie and Kira had demanded some time with her and since Niamh hadn't bothered to socialize at all since she'd been home, she knew she could only avoid them for so long. Which, in all fairness, was really *her* issue. Niamh was an introvert at heart, but once someone dragged her out of whatever cave she'd crawled into, she was usually quite happy with socializing.

Now, she had a date for a late lunch at the pub, and at the very least she should put on deodorant. She'd gone a little feral the last few days, Niamh realized with a small laugh, as she dusted off her hands on her leggings and locked up the shed. Twenty minutes later, after a quick shower, Niamh changed into slim jeans and a deep maroon cowl neck sweater. Bundling her hair in a messy knot on her head, she pulled on her faded leather jacket and left the house to walk to town.

The day was bitingly cold, but luckily no rain. In fact, Niamh wondered if they were in for snow, based on the ominous grey clouds that clung to the ridge of hills behind the village. Niamh pushed through the brightly colored doors of Gallagher's Pub, enjoying the blast of warmth that rolled over her from the cheerful fire in the corner. A bartender Niamh didn't know was behind the bar, but Niamh didn't even have a chance to go introduce herself before her name was called from a booth in the corner.

"Niamh! It's about time we dragged you out." Gracie, all vibrant eyes and sparkling beauty, waved to her from the corner. The woman fairly crackled with energy, and Niamh thought that if she ever did find a way to measure magick, then Gracie would surely break the scale. Kira, with a laid-back cool-girl vibe, was also magick but in a much more subtle manner. Niamh wondered how anyone could meet Gracie and not immediately sense her other-worldliness.

"Sorry, sorry. Sure and I get myself buried in my books, as you know." Niamh took off her coat and hung it at a post by the door before crossing the room to slide into the booth. It was the quietest part of the day, and only a few other patrons lingered over tea at their table.

"Ladies. Nice to see you all together." Cait appeared at their table, her cheeks pink from the cold, with a thick wool coat on.

"Are you working out back then?" Niamh asked.

"I am at that. Someone has to oversee the workers. But I thought I'd pop in and say hello. We've got a Guinness Stew on today and some proper mashers if you're looking for comfort food."

"That'll suit." Kira nodded and the other two agreed.

"Tea? Drinks?"

"Cider for me," Niamh decided. The other two nodded in agreement and Cait was off as fast as she'd dropped by.

"You'd think she'd slow down, but nope," Gracie said, before turning back to study Niamh. "You look well."

"Thank you. I'm actually really happy to be back. Dubs is fun, but also kind of annoying. It's loud and dirty and…loud." Niamh laughed and tucked a stray curl behind her ear. "I do miss my morning coffee spot, but I like my space here."

"How's it going with your parents? Are you in each other's way or no bother?" Kira asked.

"No bother so far. They set up a cool little lab for me in the back yard and they're both off at work all day or I'm in my lab. I can't really be complaining at all."

"Tell us what you're studying then," Gracie instructed.

"Well, I'm basically trying to measure the energy that magick produces." Niamh smiled when both of the women just stared at her. Cait arrived with their ciders and deposited them into the silence.

"What's this about?" Cait asked.

"Niamh said she's trying to measure magick. In a scientific way."

"Is that right? How so?"

"I believe magick, well, extra-sensory abilities are just a type of universal energy. And energy can be measured. They've replicated it in some photon-based experiments, but I'd like to find an easier way to measure it. I'm just not certain how yet." A glimmer of frustration slipped through Niamh and she wondered if she sounded stupid.

"And what are you hoping to prove with this?" Cait put a hand on her hip. "I thought you were going into psychology?"

"I am at that. But I very specifically want to help children with abilities like ours." Niamh lowered her voice. "However, there isn't much proof that our abilities are real. Therefore, if I can measure it in some manner, it might help take some of the stigma off of such things."

"Ah, I get it now. Smart girl." With that, Cait buzzed off to go yell at someone in the back.

"It's not a bad idea. I just wonder how you'll manage with it all." Kira pursed her lips. "For me...like how would you measure me being able to listen to an animal's thoughts? It seems like something so intangible."

"I know." Niamh plopped her chin into her hand and sighed. "Trust me. I know. That's why I think I'll start with the most basic one – telekinesis."

"I wouldn't call that basic." Gracie laughed.

"Well, it's certainly easier to measure or explain than you knitting a man's bones back together, isn't it?" Niamh raised an eyebrow at Gracie who let out another delighted laugh.

"You've the truth of it there. I wouldn't even know where to begin. Could you imagine Kira? Me walking into Niamh's class and explaining how I suck the sickness out with my hands and then direct it to something that can take it – like a piece of wood or stone - and then the stone explodes after it gets hit with the sickness? Yeah...that's just crazytown." Gracie slapped her knee and laughed once more. "I can just see it now."

"I imagine they'd have you ready to be tossed in the mental ward," Kira agreed.

"That's why I'm starting with telekinesis. And, honestly, that might be where I stop if I achieve results with it. I really just want to showcase that these abilities create measurable energy." Niamh sighed. "Perhaps I've chosen the wrong path or maybe I'm just too close to it. Maybe I should have done a slightly more traditional psychology-based project. I don't know."

"It'll all work out. You obviously have a strong interest in this and I've found that when you follow where you heart wants to take you, good things happen," Gracie promised. Her eyes grew knowing as Niamh was distracted by Mac walking into the restaurant from the back. He wore cargo work pants, a warm jacket thrown open over a plaid shirt, and had a grey knit hat tugged on over his hair.

"Speaking of..." Kira snapped her fingers in front of Niamh who whipped her head around to look at her. "You're staring."

"Oh jeez. Am I?" Niamh sighed and scrubbed a hand over her face.

"Soooo, tell us everything." Gracie pounced.

"Nothing to tell." Niamh smiled when the new server deposited their food on the table.

"Now that's a lie. Come on, Niamh. It's us. You can't hide anything from us. Nor should you. We've always got your back, remember?" Gracie said, as she scooped up a spoonful of soup and blew on it.

"Plus, we've seen the blogs. It's not like we're cut off from the world down here."

Despite herself, Niamh had also checked the gossip sites. The picture of Mac with the kids from the harbor the other night had made it into the news, which meant it was only a matter of time before reporters made their way to Grace's Cove.

"Well, the long and the short of it is that we are just friends," Niamh said as she took a sip of her crisp cider.

"Doesn't look that way to me," Kira murmured as Mac's gaze landed on their table and a wide smile lit his face as he came over to greet them.

"Niamh! How are you? Has the lab gotten all set up?" Mac asked, stopping at their table with a nod to the other women.

"I'm good, Mac. This is Gracie and Kira, family to me of sorts."

"Nice to meet you both."

"How's the building coming along?" Niamh scanned him. "You look like a proper construction guy. You just need a tool belt."

"I have one," Mac laughed as he opened his coat and

showed the tool belt that hung tightly around his hips. "It's been good. Sure and it's a learning curve, but I like it."

"A new profession then?" Niamh arched an eyebrow at him.

"You never know. It's good to diversify." Mac glanced back to where Cait stood by the back door. "I'd better get back to it before the little tyrant fires me. You still owe me that pint."

"Right," Niamh said, letting out a little whoosh of air after he disappeared from the table.

"Sooooo…" Gracie drew the word out and gave Niamh a knowing look.

"Jump him," Kira said, taking a bite of her potatoes.

"Yup," Gracie agreed. "You have to shag him."

"I do not!" Niamh's eyes widened as she hissed at the two women. "I will do no such thing."

"And why not? He was like a big golden retriever puppy all happy to see his owner. The man did everything but hump your leg," Gracie said.

"He did not. He was being friendly. We're friends. That's where it stays," Niamh insisted.

"Seems a shame," Kira shook her head sadly. "That's a ride even I'd sign up for."

"You and me both. Maybe Niamh's sight is deteriorating?" Gracie asked.

"You're both taken. With very handsome men, if I might add?" Niamh grumbled.

"What's the issue, Niamh?" Kira asked.

"It's just…I don't want to live the life he has. His every move is under a microscope. Reporters are popping out of bushes to take photos of him. Everybody wants a piece of him."

"As should you..." Gracie smiled silkily. "The prime piece."

"But…don't you see? I can't live in the public eye like that. What if…" Niamh held up her hands and gave them both a wide-eyed look. "You know."

"Ah, your gift. Sure and that's a conundrum isn't it? You wouldn't want that to be revealed publicly now, would you?" Gracie murmured.

"But surely there's a way around that," Kira argued.

"I could end up hurting his reputation or his career," Niamh said.

"I don't know about that. Seems he does enough damage on his own. Maybe if he settled down with one woman, he'd become a lot less interesting to the reporters. They're after the scandal, aren't they?" Kira pointed out.

"That's true," Gracie said. "I'm reverting back to my original opinion. Shag him."

CHAPTER 15

"*A*lright lads, that's enough for the day. Go on and have a pint then," Michael, the crew foreman, called to the three men who were currently working on converting the outdoor space outside Gallagher's Pub. Mac had found the work to be stimulating, and an easy distraction from everything that was going on. This whole week he'd gotten up early every morning, taken a brisk run and lifted weights, before he'd shown up on time at the job site. He found he liked working with his hands and was enjoying learning a new skill. The other men were tolerant with him because what he lacked in knowledge, he made up for in enthusiasm. Once they'd realized he actually wanted to work alongside them, they had welcomed him in and now he felt like one of the lads. It was a nice feeling, much like when he practiced with his team, and Mac was warming to the charm of Grace's Cove.

He'd yet to take a trip out to see this infamous cove he'd been warned away from, but with the weekend off he was hoping to convince Niamh to have a pint with him and maybe he'd get her to take him up to the cove. Unless she worked all weekend. So far, he'd been doing his best to give her the space she requested. However, Niamh was slipping into his dreams and torturing him each night. He woke up in the mornings aching for her, and his frustration at being put in the friend zone increased each day.

The kiss the other day…well, for someone who had kissed a lot of women in his life, it had been like no other. The taste of her on his lips had electrified him and he'd barely slept that night with how keyed up he'd been after-wards. If just one kiss could blow his mind like that – what would being with her do to him? All Mac knew was that he craved any time with Niamh that he could have.

"How'd you get on today, then?" Mr. Murphy, an old-timer and a regular at Gallagher's Pub since his wife passed away, nodded to Mac when he entered from the courtyard. Mac took the stool next to Mr. Murphy that the man had indicated and waited patiently as Cait automati-cally began building a pint of Guinness for him.

"I think we made some real progress today, Mr. Murphy. I can't imagine it'll be taking too much longer for the project to be finished."

"Sure and I'm glad to hear that," Cait called down to them. "What with all the banging and sawing all day."

"I hear they make these things called noise-cancelling headphones…" Mac said, earning a glare from Cait.

"Oh, boyo, not too long here and you're already bantering with Cait. She likes that, you know. She won't tell you, of course, but she likes when you've got a little spunk."

Mac eyed Mr. Murphy, who was about as placid as a lamb, and smiled.

"Sure and I'll do my best to give her a wee banter now and then." Mac nodded to a photograph on the wall behind the bar. Done in black and white, it showcased Mr. Murphy, his face lit with laughter. "That's a fine portrait of you, isn't it?"

"I'm partial to it. I'm not one for getting my picture taken, but Kira did a good job with it. It's how I hope people see me." Mr. Murphy's words held a yearning to them that spoke directly to Mac's most vulnerable spaces. He thought about the thousands of times he'd been photographed through the years. Never like this though. Mac looked at the picture once more. He agreed with Mr. Murphy – wouldn't it be nice to be seen like that and not like some womanizer who steals his mate's girl?

"You're a joy to me jaded heart, you are," Cait said as she landed on their end of the bar with two pints in hand. "Except when you're complaining about a match. That gets a touch annoying."

"Well, now, not in front of the lad, Cait. Don't want to be hurting his feelings and all." Mr. Murphy's cheeks tinged pink.

"Ah, now, no bother there. I've heard the worst of it." Mac laughed and accepted the pint from Cait. "I'm used to people complaining about our matches. I do the same when I'm watching."

"See, Cait? Mac can handle it."

"I don't doubt it. He's shown himself to be mighty capable, hasn't he? Everything alright up at the rental house then?" Cait automatically brought out a towel and began to wipe the bottles behind the bar, her eyes scanning the room. There was a lull in customers, as it was mid-afternoon, so she had time for a chat.

"That's a nice house. Same builders who are working on my center," Mr. Murphy gestured. Mac's hand was already out and catching the man's pint before it toppled over. "Well, goodness. That was a good catch, Mac. I shouldn't talk with my hands when there's such a fine pour in front of me."

Cait eyed Mac curiously, and a strange feeling washed over him, as though he was being poked at or probed. He wasn't sure he liked it. Meeting her gaze, Mac gave a little mental push and caught her eyes widening before she glanced away.

"Sure now, Mr. Murphy, haven't we discussed this? You get too excitable to be talking with your hands. Lucky to have a man with good reflexes next to you."

"It must be what makes you so good on the pitch, eh? Hell of a game, last match, wasn't it?" Mr. Murphy asked.

"It was at that." Mac took a bracing sip of his Guinness as his mind whirled. What was going on here? There was something more to Cait, and he wasn't sure what it was. He'd rarely felt such a physical manifestation of otherness, and yet it was like he could feel Cait all but massaging his mind with her hands. It was odd, deeply unsettling, and he needed answers. But since she wasn't inclined to speak on what she'd seen Mac do to catch Mr. Murphy's drink, Mac supposed he should offer her the same courtesy.

"You'll be in fine shape for next season if you keep up with the builder work. It's a demanding job. A good one, too. Honest day's work," Mr. Murphy continued and Mac pulled his head back into the conversation.

"I like it. But…tell me more about this center of yours. What do you mean?"

"Oh, right, you wouldn't know. I'm having my house turned into a community center of sorts. A space for the elderly to go play cards or learn a skill while also having some options for the youth. There's a great yard behind it so we can set up an area for games, that kind of thing. Plus, it energizes us old-timers to be around the kids and help them out. It's a win-win, I guess."

"It's a grand idea, Mr. Murphy. Everyone's really excited about it," Cait said, as she held a bottle up to the light and wiped it down.

"You'll have to come by and see it sometime," Mr. Murphy said to Mac.

"I'd like that. Do you plan to teach any rugby classes to the kids?" Mac asked.

"Maybe. If you're interested in offering up a lesson or two, I'm sure every lad from age five to fifty would be there." Mr. Murphy laughed and slapped the bar.

"And more than a few women as well," Cait mused.

"What's this I heard about you not being allowed to date the women here?" Mr. Murphy asked.

"Ah…" Mac said. Where had Mr. Murphy heard that? Apparently, Niamh wasn't wrong about this town being full of gossips.

"Is that true? I think I might know who gave that order…" Cait shot Mac a knowing look that made him want to squirm on his stool.

"Oh, are you and sweet Niamh an item then?" Mr.

Murphy asked and Mac's eyes widened. He held up hand to stop Mr. Murphy from going down that path before it was all over Grace's Cove that he fancied Niamh.

He did, of course. But Mac didn't need the whole town to know that.

"Niamh and I are friends. However, because she helped me out of the tough situation I'm dealing with in Dublin, she had a few instructions for me when it came to navigating my stay here."

"She told you that we're a bunch of gossips, didn't she?" Cait leaned on the bar and laughed.

"She might have mentioned something to that effect, I can't be certain," Mac tactfully agreed.

"She's not wrong. We are. But we also have everyone's back. So, double-edged sword, I suppose." Cait shrugged.

"Did you really kiss your friend's woman?" Mr. Murphy's voice was serious and Mac found that he didn't want to ruin Mr. Murphy's opinion of him.

"I did not. Well, there was a kiss as you can see from the photos." Mac sighed and took a sip of his beer. "But she ambushed me. She's mad at Fintan and wanting to make him jealous. I was just her best ammunition."

"Well, now, that's unfortunate. Did you talk to him about it?" Mr. Murphy asked.

"I did. I went straight back inside and told him what happened before any of it hit the news."

"That's a good lad. Address it right away. Did he take it well or not so much?" Mr. Murphy asked.

"Not so well at that moment, but he was several pints in. We've texted about it a few times since and he seems to be in a better frame of mind now. Not sure what will happen with his relationship with Kristie, but that's not my problem unless she uses me for her own purposes again."

"That has to be tough," Mr. Murphy said, kindness shining in his eyes. "It's an unfair portrayal of you in the public light. And you can probably protest all you want, but those reporters just print the best story, don't they?"

"That they do." Mac was oddly touched by Mr. Murphy's immediate support.

"So, Niamh tells you not to date any women here. Is it because she wants you to herself or because she is protecting your reputation and wants to make sure you don't get in any more trouble?" Mr. Murphy tapped a finger to his lips in consideration while Mac's mouth dropped open.

"I…I can't really say on that one, Mr. Murphy." And he wasn't going to say what his hope was, no he most certainly was not. Because if he gave any indication what-soever that he had interest in Niamh, it seemed like the whole town would be watching them with a magnifying glass.

"She's a lovely girl, isn't she?" Mr. Murphy asked.

"She is very nice. Niamh has been a good friend to me. Her parents are also very nice. Well, once her father and I squared things away."

"Heard he landed one right on your eye." Mr. Murphy gestured to him with his pint.

"Patrick has a mean right hook, doesn't he?" Cait laughed and finished wiping the last of the bottles in the rail in front of her. "Not the best welcome to Grace's Cove, but I can see where he was coming from."

"I don't blame him for it in the slightest," Mac

laughed. "I would likely have done the same if I had only heard the information the news stories had presented."

"Well, it's grand you worked things out. Heard you were going to dinner there as well?" Cait asked.

"Yes, Mrs. Kearney has been kind enough to invite me when she's cooking. She says she doesn't want me to feel lonely up in the house by myself." Mac shrugged one shoulder and finished his pint. "I guess she doesn't know that I'm used to being on my own."

"You don't have to be any more, if you don't want to be. We're here." Mr. Murphy met his eyes and then raised his chin to Cait who nodded her agreement. The truth of his statement sent warmth careening through Mac and he found himself getting oddly choked up. Swallowing quickly, he put a smile on his face.

"I had a strong feeling I would like Grace's Cove. Thank you for making me feel welcome."

"Another one, Mac?" Cait held up his empty glass.

"No, thank you. I've a bit of paperwork to go through still today."

"There's music on for later – a band in from Dublin. You'll want to come back down to get dinner before it starts." It was more of an order than an invitation.

"Yes, ma'am."

ONCE MAC LEFT, Cait turned to Mr. Murphy.

"He's searching for home," Mr. Murphy said.

"He is at that. And...something else," Cait smiled. Bending over, she hauled a leather book out and plopped it on the counter of the bar. "I'm opening bets for Niamh and Mac."

"Well, now, we can't be certain the lad likes her." Mr. Murphy tugged on the rim of his newsboy cap. "He claims they are just friends."

"When was the last time a man followed a woman clear across the country to spend time in her hometown and just wanted to be friends?"

"Sure and that's a good point. I'm in for twenty…" Mr. Murphy reached for his wallet.

CHAPTER 16

*M*ac strolled down the hill from his house, the wind biting into his shoulders, the lights of Grace's Cove like little fireflies dotting the dark hills. He didn't mind the cold, as some did, for it often energized him. Tonight was one of those nights, and a little hum of anticipation rushed through him at the thought of a live band.

Well, at least that is what he told himself.

He'd texted Niamh, asking her to join him for a pint and some music tonight. Mac had wanted to call her and properly invite her out as his date, but he was doing his best to not interfere with her lab time, so he sent a text message instead. Turns out, she was already meeting the two women he'd met the other day at the pub. Mac supposed it was hard to date in this town where the main pub was where everyone went to hang out. More or less, you were going to run into your crush one way or the other, Mac mused.

Already he could hear the chatter of voices and

laughter as the door swung open from Gallagher's Pub. It was nice, Mac realized, to know he didn't have to skip a line or be on some VIP list to get through the door. Instead, he knew he could walk inside and see a few friendly faces that he'd met over the past week. The appeal of small towns was beginning to reveal itself to him. Mac held the door for an elderly woman who toddled out of the pub, nodding to her politely as she smiled up at him.

"Now, Sarah. There's a strapping lad if I've ever seen one. You could make a play for him, you know."

"Nan, you know I'm engaged." A pretty young woman flashed Mac an apologetic smile and hooked an arm through her Nan's and all but dragged the woman down the street.

"Then you're not married yet, are you?" Nan turned around and blew Mac a kiss and he threw back his head and laughed. Gone were the days where he had super-models falling in his lap. He much preferred this type of friendly flirtation, if he had his say.

Mac stepped inside the pub and scanned the room, smiling when Mr. Murphy waved to him from the bar. He didn't see Niamh yet, so he made his way across the pub, nodding his hello to a few people who called to him. No wonder Cait needed more space, Mac thought as he stopped at the empty stool by Mr. Murphy. The pub was packed, standing room only, and nobody seemed to mind it one bit. Everyone from babies to grandmothers were packed into booths and tables, while a group of lads stood and discussed the football.

"I saved you a seat as I knew it would be busy tonight.

This band's a popular one, it is." Mr. Murphy tugged at his cap and his smile made his whole face crinkle up.

"Well, I'm lucky to have you as a friend, then. There's standing room only it seems." Mac took his coat off and tossed it across the back of his stool before taking a seat. He nodded to Cait who pointed at the Guinness tap and then turned back to look at the patrons of the pub.

"It'll be like that all night. Nobody seems to mind. I think Cait's done her best to maximize space here, but I know the courtyard will be a welcome addition. It's been well-used in the summers. But making it winter-proof is a smart move."

"It's not far off from being done. It will definitely add some space for people to move about."

"What will you do once it's done? Head back to Dubs, I suppose? I mean, you'll need to get back to training, won't you?" Mr. Murphy accepted the pint that Cait slid to him.

"How's it going then, Mac? All good?"

"I'm good, thanks."

"Are you needing a meal tonight or just drinks?"

"Just drinks is fine. I heated up a frozen pizza at home." Mac grinned at her baleful look and raised his pint in a toast when she huffed off.

"Nothing wrong with a frozen pizza," Mr. Murphy said. "I told Cait she should start serving late-night pizza and she told me to shove it."

"Is there any late-night food here? I was under the impression that it shut down after dark." Mac sipped his Guinness, enjoying the creamy stout, and relaxed a bit.

"Sure and there's a chippy around the corner that has

some easy late-night eats. Otherwise, none to be found really. At least the bakery is open early. The fishermen can grab a pasty or two on the way to the docks."

"Ah, there's the band now." Mac nodded to where a man came in from the back carrying a guitar.

"And there's Niamh." Before Mac could turn, Mr. Murphy was already calling her over.

Mac swallowed against his suddenly dry throat. She looked…decadent, he decided. There was something about the way she dressed, as though she really loved the clothes she was wearing, that drew all eyes in the room to her. It wasn't that she was even wearing the latest fashions, at least there were no name brands that Mac could see on her clothes, but it was how she put herself together.

Niamh wore a long-sleeved velvet dress in deep teal with little fringes at the arms and at the hem that ended mid-thigh and just short of her patent-leather boots. The boots…they made Mac's pulse race as he thought about tracing his hand up the shiny leather to the soft skin of her inner thigh. He quickly gulped his Guinness and pulled his eyes away lest he stare too long.

"Hi." Niamh smacked two loud kisses on each of Mr. Murphy's cheeks. Her hair was teased and tumbled wildly around her head and Mac wanted to dive his hands into it and pull her close for a different kind of kiss.

"There's a lovely lass." Mr. Murphy turned to raise a finger to Cait. "Cider for you?"

"I'm thinking a whiskey to start actually. Green Spot for me, please." Niamh smiled up at Mac, momentarily taking his breath away.

"You look nice," Niamh said, and Mac glanced down to his heather grey long-sleeve and dark denim pants.

"Thank you. They were the only clean clothes I had left," Mac smiled. "However, you look positively smashing. Really, Niamh. Just…wow."

"Thank you, that's a nice compliment. I love this dress and haven't had much time to wear it. But, I figured for a band – why not? I heard they're making a name for themselves in Dublin, so it'll be a busy one tonight."

"You can have my seat," Mac said, standing and gesturing to his stool.

"Thank you," Niamh slid onto the stool and crossed her legs, causing Mac to instantly regret his decision as a pale flash of thigh showed above those boots.

Those boots were going to haunt him.

Tearing his eyes away, he caught a twinkle in Mr. Murphy's eyes, and just shook his head slightly to discourage wherever the old man's thoughts were going.

"Oh there's Gracie and Kira. With Brogan and Dylan." Niamh waved to them and turned to look up at Mac. "You'll like their partners. Dylan is a developer 'King of the Universe' business guy and Brogan just opened a nature center up in the hills by the cove. Wildly different, but they get on like they've known each other forever."

Mac smiled through the introductions, sizing the men up and finding them both to be easy-going and likeable, and soon the group had commandeered enough stools that they had the small corner of the bar for their own.

"You missing city-life at all?" Dylan asked, leaning over so Mac could hear him as the band tuned their instruments.

"Not at the moment, no. I haven't been here long enough to miss it, I guess. This place has a certain charm to it, I won't lie."

"Careful, then. Grace's Cove has a way of digging her hooks into you. You'll find it harder and harder to leave the longer you stay." What should have sounded like a warning instead intrigued Mac. Wouldn't it be nice to have a place to call home? He didn't particularly enjoy going back to where he grew up, for his father remained disinterested unless he gave him money, and the rest of the town didn't seem to know how to speak to him anymore. Fame had set him apart from the working-class families there, and instead of making him feel welcomed home, he just felt awkwardly like an outsider. Perhaps it was his own issue, as he'd spent every waking moment trying to figure out a way out of there. If he visited Grace's Cove again, would he finally be able to view home in a different light?

"I'll need to get back for training at some point. But right now? It's a nice spot to land."

"I hear you're into construction now. I have a few crews that are hiring…" Dylan laughed when Gracie smacked him.

"The man is a professional athlete. He's not going to come work for your crew." Gracie rolled her eyes. "I swear this man is always working."

"It was just an offer, my love. In case he was looking for a career change." Dylan pressed a kiss to the top of Gracie's head. Their casual intimacy twisted at Mac's heart. Had he ever been that comfortable with a partner before?

"Not before he comes to teach rugby at the center,

Dylan. Back off my boyo, here. I claimed him first." Mr. Murphy held up a threatening fist and Dylan put two hands in the air, pretending to be scared.

"Are you going to do that?" Niamh turned to him, her stormy eyes lit with interest. "Teach the kids, that is? Is that something you want to do?"

"I mean…yes, actually. It is something I'd like to do. I just haven't figured out what that looks like yet." Mac shrugged at the surprise on her face. "I still have some things to figure out where that is concerned."

"What's there to figure out? Come down to the center. Run a few drills. No big deal." Mr. Murphy shrugged and Mac grinned. Maybe it could be as simple as that. At least to start. Not everything had to be formalized and put to a grand scale.

"It's pissing rain every day. Where is he running drills?" Gracie demanded.

"That's a fair point. Well, one of these days when it's clear. You just put the word out. People will show up, I promise you that," Mr. Murphy said. "Doesn't need to be a formal thing."

The band launched into their first song, the music drowning out any conversation, and Mac relaxed against the bar, happy to not have any further discussion into what it is he wanted to do with coaching. It felt like with every moment he spent around Niamh and her friends, more of his defenses were peeled away, revealing things about himself that he wasn't yet ready to share with the world. It wasn't just fame that made him cautious about sharing more of himself with others.

It was that he'd always had to hide – to protect himself

– from what other people might think of him. Of what he could do. His glance slid to Niamh, her eyes alight with excitement as she all but vibrated in her stool. She clearly wanted to dance. Without thinking too much about it, he reached for her arm.

"Care to dance?"

"You dance?" Niamh's eyes lit up.

"Sure do," Mac said. "Let's see if you can keep up in those boots."

"Oh, bring it on – pretty boy."

CHAPTER 17

The band – a fusion of Irish and rock – switched to an upbeat Celtic song with the fiddle taking a lead and the drums sending a pulsing beat through the crowd. In moments, dancers had paired off and the dance floor came alive as people challenged each other to keep up as the beat increased. Niamh laughed, tossing her hair over her shoulder, and sent him a challenging look.

Lifting his chin, Mac met her head on when she dove into a complicated dance step. Linking his arm through hers, he swung her into a spin and then reeled her back in so that her body pressed hotly against his for a moment. Lust shot straight through him, warming his core, and Mac spun her once more wanting the touch of her against him again.

"Sure and you do have rhythm then," Niamh shouted over the music, when he drew her close. "I thought a big lad like you would stumble all over himself."

"Don't tell anyone," Mac leaned close to whisper in her ear, "but I've taken dance lessons before."

"Have you really?" Niamh's eyes lit up when his hands came to her waist and he drew her into a complicated series of steps. The drums picked up speed, pulsing through them, and the crowd cheered as the singer wailed into the microphone. "I'm guessing for a girlfriend?"

"Nope." Mac laughed down at her. "For rugby."

"Well, now that's just silly. How can dance and rugby have anything in common?" Niamh shouted. The way her body moved – and felt – under the velvet of her dress was driving Mac mad. He kept his hands at her waist, though he wanted to stroke them up her back, and lower, to cup the soft curve of her bum under his hand.

"It's a dance, you see?" Mac said, his mouth at her ear. "Rugby isn't just about the strongest man winning. It's also about being agile. Anticipating the player's next move. Working in tandem with your team. Just like…"

"Dancing with your partner," Niamh said breathlessly, and she almost undid him when she licked her lower lip subconsciously. He stared, wanting nothing more than to lean in and have a taste.

To savor her.

Instead, as the song neared its end, he pushed her out – surprising her with the move – and then pulled her back in before dipping her with a delightful flourish on the song's last note. Swinging her back up, Niamh's hair flew around her head and she laughed in delight at Mac. Unbeknownst to them, the crowd had formed a little circle around the two and now everyone clapped for them.

The moment hung suspended between them, Mac's eyes on Niamh's, laughter and something so much heavier in the air around them. For a moment, the chattering voices, the music…everything faded away and all he saw was her. This woman – she could be the one for him. See him for who he really was. For the first time ever, Mac wanted to share all of himself with another.

Niamh blinked at him, as though reading his intentions, and then the moment was broken by a squeal from across the dance floor.

"Mac!"

Mac glanced up to see three stunning women – easily models – push through the crowd to him. Already, Niamh had sized the women up and was pulling her hands from his.

"Wait, Niamh," Mac said, but she was already leaving. Leaving him behind because this was his life – constantly being accosted by others.

"I'm going for my drink," Niamh said, shooting him a polite smile that didn't reach her eyes. It infuriated him; the way she gave him this look as though he was just a friendly stranger to her.

"We didn't know you'd be here!" One of the women, a willowy blonde with obvious breast implants latched onto his arm without asking. "We just thought we'd come on the tour with Derek."

"This night certainly got more interesting." This from a dark-haired sinewy beauty.

"I'd say. Though there's a few cuties in the crowd tonight. I bet we'll be having ourselves loads of fun tonight." The red head gave him a practiced sulky pout.

A bone-deep exhaustion leached through Mac. There had been a time in his life when women like this crowding around him had seemed like the crowning point of his life.

More times than he could count, he'd found himself back home with one or another of them only to find them more interested in posting pictures with him to their social media than actually having some semblance of a conversation with him. Not all – many of them had been more than happy to jump right into bed with him – but Mac now found the idea of that distasteful as well.

He realized that he'd rather sleep alone than next to someone who barely knew his name.

"Ladies, do I know you?" Mac asked, pulling his arm away from the blonde who clung to him like a burr.

"My friend Sheena made out with you once," the red head offered with her little pout.

"Right. Well, welcome to Grace's Cove. I'm sure you'll enjoy yourselves. I'm going…" Mac didn't know where he was going. Just not on the dance floor with these three.

"Mac, can you get us drinks? We're positively parched."

An escape. Mac nodded and pushed his way through the crowd, not bothering to ask what the women drank. With those types it was always either champagne or vodka soda as they were inevitably always watching their calorie intake. When he finally made his way back to Mr. Murphy's side, his annoyance had reached peak level.

"Old friends?" Mr. Murphy asked.

"Never met them." Mac pressed his lips in a line as he turned to look for Niamh. Cait arrived behind the bar.

"Pint for me please. Three vodka sodas or champagne. Whichever you have and is easier." Cait raised an eyebrow at him.

"Put it on my tab but please have someone deliver them to three stick-thin self-obsessed women in the middle of the room. I'll tip extra for the delivery fee as I know you're slammed."

"Don't want to take them yourself then?" Cait asked, already mixing the drinks.

"Nope. You couldn't pay me to go back over and talk to them."

"Good, I expected better of you. I'm glad to see I won't be disappointed." Cait nodded and, grabbing the drinks in her hands, ducked neatly under the passthrough.

"Not going back to your women?" Gracie asked at his elbow and he looked down at her, a flash of annoyance in his eyes.

"They're not my women. I don't even know them." Mac turned to see the women scanning the pub to look for him. "Where did Niamh go?"

"She left. Said she's got work in the morning and it's late."

"Is that really why she left?" Mac wasn't sure what made him so bold, but he felt like a dying man who needed a drop of water...anything to make him survive. He needed to know if Niamh cared, at all, about him. For a moment, on the dance floor, he was convinced that she did. Then she'd shuttered the emotions in her eyes and slipped neatly away the minute the consequences of his fame had slapped him in the face.

Once again.

"That's what she said," Gracie shrugged.

"I'm going to be outside." Mac could see the women were already heading for him, so he grabbed the pint that

Cait had put in front of him and disappeared into the back hallway. Grateful that the construction tape was up and that nobody would be back there, Mac slipped through the back door and into the cool night air. Without a coat, the wind was biting, but Mac didn't care. The cold helped him to calm his frustration down.

"Checking out your handiwork?"

Mac turned to find Cait leaning in the doorway.

"Something like that. I'm just taking in some air. Don't let me take you away from your busy night. It's a mad crush in there." Mac turned around again and took a sip of his beer, studying one of the walls he had helped to build the other day.

"I'm on a break." Cait stepped forward, letting the door swing closed behind her, neatly cutting out the sounds of the pub. "Something on your mind?"

Mac shrugged one shoulder, non-committal.

"I mean…from a casual observer's standpoint, it seems like you were having a lot of fun dancing with Niamh. And then three leggy beauties showed up and she hightailed it out here. So, what's up there?"

"Nothing. I don't know them." Mac sighed and ran a hand over his neck to diffuse some tension that knotted there. "But it's the same everywhere. I used to love that attention…well, to a point. The gossip magazines weren't wrong in what they printed about me. It's what I thought I needed to do, I guess. It was what fame was…well, is… right? Everyone wants to be the guy at the club with all the women, all the flash, all the money. That's when you know you've made it, right?"

"I wouldn't know." Cait stepped forward so she was

shoulder to shoulder with him, looking out at her courtyard. "I never wanted that life."

"I'm not sure that I did either."

"Then why did you go for it?"

"Because rugby is the only place where life makes sense to me. It's the only home I've ever had. Fame came with it." Mac couldn't bring himself to look at Cait in the quiet of the courtyard. She was a stand-up woman and an excellent boss, but perhaps it was a touch too soon to confide in her like this. He hoped he hadn't overstepped his boundaries.

"I understand wanting to build something for yourself. Something of your own – that *you* made." Cait gestured out to the courtyard. "I've been building my home for years now. And I take care of it. I nurture it. Gallagher's Pub is the heart of me – but it also doesn't define me. I'm more than just the pub. We are all more than just our job."

"What if I don't know what that looks like? What if…" Mac paused as he tried to think about what to say next. "What if I've always felt like there was more to me than anybody really saw?"

"More than your ability as a world-famous rugby player?" Cait asked. "There's quite a lot to be said for your talent, Mac. I wouldn't dismiss it."

"I'm not. But I just…there's more. There's more to me."

"Ah." Cait nodded. "I think you'll find there's a lot of people in Grace's Cove who share your…sentiments."

"What does that even mean?" Confusion…and something like hope slipped through Mac.

"I'm saying that…if you allow it…the right people *will*

see you. But that's a choice you have to make. That you have to be open to."

"I'm not sure I know how." Mac's words were barely a whisper.

"Ah, well, you've only to ask for help, Mac. Just think on that when you're ready."

"Cait?" The door opened. "Is there a new case of pint glasses? I can't find them."

"Coming." Cait turned and patted his arm, her eyes knowing in the light from the courtyard lantern. "You get to decide what your life looks like, Mac. Nobody else. Remember that."

With that, Cait swept inside, leaving Mac with an unsettled heart and a mind whirling with questions.

CHAPTER 18

*M*ac texted Niamh the next morning and asked her if she wanted to drive out to the cove with him later that day. For the first time in days, the sunshine was peeking through the clouds and Mac needed to work off some of his anxious energy from the night before. He'd wanted to contact Niamh when he'd gotten back to the rental house, just to make sure she was okay, but once he'd glanced at the clock, he'd realized it was quite late. Mac had ended up staying for a few more pints, studiously ignoring the models, making sure that nobody in the pub could question what his intentions were. He wanted it known that he didn't just take off with any pretty face that walked into a pub and that he was sticking by Niamh's request that he not date while he was in Grace's Cove. Granted, she'd said not to date her friends – but Mac wasn't willing to screw up there. At the end of the night, when he'd left alone, Cait had shot him a look of approval on the way out the door. That one look had warmed him the whole way home, and he hoped that the word would get back to Niamh that he hadn't given those women any of his time.

Mac waited for an hour after he sent his message, working his way through several sets of weightlifting, before he gave up on waiting on Niamh. After a quick shower, Mac dressed for the outdoors in sturdy boots, several layers for warmth, and a sturdy rain slicker. Tugging his grey knit cap on his head, he grabbed a backpack and loaded it with water, snacks, and a book. It wasn't often he got a chance to wander in nature alone, and maybe he'd find a nice spot to get out of his head for a while.

The right people will see you.

Cait's words from last night echoed in his mind as he took to the winding road that hugged the cliffs on the drive out of the village toward the cove. Mac realized that he wanted Niamh to see him. She was the right person. He couldn't yet understand his fascination with her – not really. Of course, she was beautiful. But it was more than that. So much more. Not only did she have brains, but it was probably her compassionate heart that was doing him in more than anything else. She just…she cared. She *actually* cared about Mac finding his way and then gave him the space to do so. It still irked him that she believed that he had purposely kissed Kristie. Annoyance flared through him and Mac grimaced as he took a turn a touch too tightly and the rocky wall of the cliff scratched against the front panel of his SUV.

"Damn it," Mac hissed. He should know better than to take a big car on tiny Irish roads. Particularly ones where the cliffs fell away to the ocean on one side of the road. He needed to get out of his head and pay attention to his driving. It really was a stunning area, Mac thought, as he slowed the SUV and focused on the landscape around him. All sharp cliffs, moody winter seas, and bulbous white clouds dotting the sky – it was certainly striking. He imagined in the summer that this road would be crowded with cars taking in the beautiful scenery, but today he had it to himself.

Mac followed the directions that Mr. Murphy had been kind enough to provide, remarking that the village of Grace's Cove had taken down the actual sign that used to point to where the cove was located. Apparently, they really did want to discourage people from visiting the beach. Mr. Murphy had also warned him about going into the cove and Mac had nodded, recounting the same warnings from Niamh's parents. The people here really were superstitious, Mac mused, as he turned the SUV off the main road that led to a little stone cottage higher up in the hills and bumped along the dirt path until he came across a lone picnic table.

This must be the spot, Mac thought, and turned the SUV off. Getting out of the car, he stretched, and then grabbed his backpack from the backseat. Sliding the straps over his shoulders, Mac circumvented the table and went to stand by the little gate that had been erected at the top of the path that wound down the side of the cliff to the sandy beach far below.

For a moment, Mac lost his breath. A wave of dizziness washed over him, and he took two steps back just in case he lost his head and toppled over the edge of the cliff.

Steeling himself, Mac took several deeps breaths in and stepped forward again.

The cove itself was stunning. Craggy rock walls jutted proudly into the wintry sky, forming almost a perfect circle over the water, but leaving a small entry for a boat. A wide stretch of sandy beach beckoned, and the path switch-backed across the cliff walls, making it look to be an easier climb than he had first thought it would be. Mac under-stood why people were drawn to explore this spot.

It wasn't the beauty of nature that struck him so heavily and forced him once more to take a step back. Oh no. There was most definitely something else there that…well, it called to him. Mac reached out and trailed a finger through the air, wondering if it was all in his mind. The air felt thick here, like a veil, and he waved his hand again, feeling tendrils of… otherness…curl around him. What was this place? Despite the warnings that he'd been given, Mac stepped forward.

A bark startled him, and Mac glanced over to see an Irish setter barreling across the field to him, her tongue lolling from her mouth. From the cottage, Mac assumed, and looked up to where the house sat. He couldn't see anyone out in the field, but clearly this was a happy and well-taken-care-of dog.

"Hey." Mac bent and gave the dog a rub, and she happily flipped on her back and exposed her stomach for Mac to scratch. "Aren't you a doll?" After a few more moments of indulging the dog, Mac straightened.

"Time for me to go, girl. Go on then. Head on home." Mac didn't want the dog to follow him into the cove and risk falling from the path or something. Granted, the dog was probably used to clambering all over these hills, but he'd be beside himself if the animal got hurt. "Go on now."

The dog, seeming to understand his intentions, whined at the gate to the path. Mac stepped over the gate, leaving the dog neatly on the other side, and patted her head once more. "I'll be fine. I'm just worried about you. Go on home now."

Instead, the dog sat, whining occasionally, as Mac began the trek down to the water. Soon, the winds were louder than the dog's whine, and Mac lost himself in the peacefulness of the hike down to the water. It had been ages since he'd taken himself on a proper hike, and now he wondered why he didn't make more time for it. Hiking was good exercise and it gave him a proper chance to get away from his phone, his computer, and any other way that people could reach him.

Mac hummed to himself as he reached the bottom of the path. For a moment, he just stood there, taking in the awe-inspiring sight of the massive cliffs hugging the beach. It was as if the entire world had faded away, and he alone was left in the universe. Not a bad spot to have a good think about life, Mac mused and stepped out onto the sand.

For a moment, it was impossible for him to move forward and Mac froze, confusion lancing through him. What in the world was going on? He pushed again, and then, as though he was stepping through almost a membrane of sorts, Mac was finally free to step forward.

"That was odd," Mac muttered, turning in a full circle and looking at the empty cliffs above him. The water, a stormy grey-blue, roiled at the shoreline. Testing himself, Mac took one step and then another step forward, but the weird sensation of having to push through something didn't return. Perhaps he had just imagined it?

It was quieter here, Mac realized, as he began to stroll the beach. Birds swooped lazily far above him, but none landed on the beach or picked through the tide pools. Curious, he walked over to one of the tide pools and crouched, watching as a small crab scuttled away from him.

"I wonder how you can be here."

Mac almost toppled face-first into the tidal pool. He caught himself, scraping his hand on a sharp edge of rock, and then stood. Bringing his bloody hand to his lips, Mac turned and his eyebrows shot straight to his hairline.

"Uh…" Mac's bloody hand dropped away from his mouth as he stared at what he was quite certain was a ghost.

"Yes, that's right, I'm a spirit. Really though, who are you?" The spirit, faintly glowing in the daylight, looked like a woman with flowing white hair and she was holding a puppy.

"Uh…" Mac repeated. He turned in a full circle again. Yup, he was definitely still in the cove and until a moment ago, he had been alone.

"Were you not gifted with the ability to speak?" The woman asked, stroking her dog as she tilted her head at him in question.

"Sure and I can speak, but it's a bit of a shock it is to speak to a spirit is all," Mac finally said.

"My name is Fiona. I used to live here. Well, I still do. Just not in my human form."

Mac gulped at that. Fear trickled through him and he wondered if he'd lost his mind or if this was some trick they played to punk the tourists that came to the cove. How they'd execute a trick of that nature he wasn't exactly sure. He took a hesitant step back, and then paused when the roar of waves crashing sounded behind him.

"I wouldn't step any further back. The cove doesn't seem to mind you are here, for whatever reason, yet it's best not to anger her."

"Oh...kay?" Mac drew the word out. He froze in place and just looked at Fiona, his mouth gaping open. "I have no idea what to do right now."

"Well, sure and you can start by answering some of my questions, can't you?"

"Um, I don't know how to answer them?" Mac's voice went up at the end of the sentence. "I can tell you that my name is Mac. I can't answer why I'm allowed to be here or whatever your question was about the cove. Because I don't rightly know the answer to that."

"That's a fair answer then." Fiona snuggled the puppy closer in her arms, resting her chin on its head, and studied Mac carefully. "You've heard about the cove at least? Why you shouldn't be here?"

"I was told it was enchanted and they warn tourists away."

"Ah, so you did the ritual to get in." Fiona nodded as though her question was finally answered.

"Um, no. Sure and I didn't do any ritual. I don't know what you mean..." Mac shrugged helplessly.

"So, you're telling me then that you just hiked down

the path and walked out onto the beach with no problem at all?"

"Well…" Mac thought about the weird wall he'd walked through. "I guess there was this one part that was weird. Aside from me having delusions and talking to a ghost that is."

"That part is real. Go on." Fiona waved him on as though they were having a simple chat about the news over a pint.

"It just felt like…when I got to the beach…like I walked through something. A wall of sorts. But not. In the air." Mac gestured lamely, unsure how to describe it.

"You stepped through the veil. Without harm. And you could feel the veil?"

"I…sure. If that's what you're calling it?" Mac's pulse rocketed. Didn't stepping through the veil mean he was dead? Had he died? Was he a ghost as well? Desperately, he looked down at his hands. Still flesh that he could see. "Am I dead?"

"No, of course not. It's what you are exactly that has me curious."

"Myself as well." Mac whirled as another voice greeted him.

"Gracie?" Relief poured through him at the sight of Niamh's friend walking across the sand, a tartan shawl wound around her shoulders.

"Aye. Rosie came and got me. She wasn't happy that you'd gone into the cove."

"Is that your dog?"

"It is. She's a brilliant companion. And she doesn't like when people go to the cove – particularly unattended.

Most get hurt here, you know. And, then I have to take care of them." Gracie brushed back a lock of hair that blew into her face.

"I don't. Not really. I'm…you're real, right?" Mac looked to Gracie and then back to the ghost, not sure if Gracie could see her.

"I am."

"He's thinking he's lost his mind because he's seeing ghosts." Fiona pursed her lips and sighed. "I'm wondering why he's here. And why the cove likes him. He says he walked through the veil without a ritual."

"Who are you, Mac?" Gracie trailed closer, tilting her head to look up at him. "Are you kin to us then?"

"I…I don't think that I am."

"MacGregor." Fiona continued to purse her lips and think. "Gracie, you would know better than anyone. Did you have a MacGregor in your bloodline?"

"Why would that matter exactly?" Mac's heart was hammering in his chest and he felt rooted to the spot, waiting to watch this play out…however it was meant to.

"I see you weren't given the actual reason why you can't visit the cove."

"I was told it was enchanted." Mac now realized that Niamh had not been straightforward with him.

"But were you told why? Never mind," Gracie waved it away. "The long and the short of it is that the cove is enchanted, and a family's bloodline was given powers. Extra-sensory abilities. Healing skills. That kind of thing."

Mac's mouth went dry.

"What family?" Mac asked softly.

"Well, mine of course." Gracie grinned widely at him.

"And, since this is a sacred space, well, only family can come here unscathed or if you understand the ritual that goes with it. So...I wonder?"

"I don't sense his bloodline," Fiona whispered to Gracie as though Mac wasn't there. "He's not one of us."

"How in the world..." Mac stopped speaking. If he was really standing here talking to a woman cradling a ghost-puppy, he guessed anything was possible. She could probably sniff his blood. The thought turned his stomach a bit, so he pushed that out of his mind.

"Dillon's daughter..." Gracie's eyes went wide. "Of course."

"Oh, Gracie. Did you give her powers? You've a heart of gold, you do."

"I remember now..." Gracie turned to Fiona, cutting Mac neatly from the conversation and he debated briefly whether he should make a run for it. Except for the fact that he was, you know, frozen in place and all. "I'll admit, it's a bit of a blur through the decades now. But I meant for the enchantment to include those that I loved. Dillon...that is the man that I loved and lost in that time, well, I later found out a daughter was born to him while he was at sea. He never knew. I wonder if my enchantment extended to her because of my fierce love for Dillon?" Both women turned back to study Mac.

"I'm really confused," Mac finally said. Gracie was talking as though she was the same person from centuries ago – apparently the very one who had enchanted the cove. Which would make her...well, hell, maybe he was delusional?

"Ah, well, again, it's worth investigating. My daughter

gave birth on this beach." Gracie laughed as Mac's eyes widened. "My daughter in another lifetime. Her father, well, I once loved him. Fiercely. I'm wondering if you're of his line. Perhaps the enchantment bled through so-to-speak."

"Right, of course." About a thousand questions rushed into Mac's mind, but he just stood there gaping at Gracie.

"At the moment…it's the only thing that makes sense. Which means…" Surprise lit Gracie's eyes. "That you likely have powers as well. Do you?"

"I…" Mac's mouth dropped open. Never once in his life had he spoken about what he could do. Not to a single soul. And now he stood, his world blown up, on the enchanted beach of Grace's Cove and looked his future dead in the face.

"Aye, I do."

CHAPTER 19

*W*hat had she told the man about going into the cove? Niamh paced the house, continuing to glance down at the phone in her hand, worry turning knots in her stomach. She pictured Mac, his body lying broken on the beach, and she was just reaching for the car keys when her phone sounded with a text.

He's fine.

Gracie didn't elaborate and Niamh didn't really care. Relief swept through her and she put the keys down. Blowing out a breath, Niamh walked through the empty house to the kitchen and put on the kettle to heat water for tea. The night before flashed back to her and she grimaced, annoyed with Mac, and at herself, for responding the way she had.

Dancing with Mac had been…intoxicating. Their rhythm had matched and for a moment the pub had faded into the background, and it had just been the two of them – suspended in that moment. Yet every time she allowed herself to think, for even a moment, that they might have something together, she was slapped in the face by the reality of his life. This time in the form of some devastatingly beautiful women. Models, probably. Niamh sniffed and poured the hot water into her cup before turning to rummage for a biscuit.

She'd already had several text messages informing her that Mac had stayed at the pub and hadn't left with any of the women. Niamh had promptly replied to each stating that she and Mac were just friends and he was free to do as he wished. Hopefully that would quash any potential rumors that might have flared up after their dance. Niamh blew out a breath and leaned against the counter, her mug of tea warming her hands. Could she blame anyone really? That dance had been *hot*.

The front door opened and Morgan hummed her way inside the house, stopping short when she saw Niamh in the kitchen.

"It still surprises me to see you here sometimes!" Morgan laughed, putting her hand to her chest. "Quiet as a mouse you are."

"Sorry about that. My own mind was wandering." Niamh gestured with her mug. "So I came in for a cuppa."

"Ah, what's bothering you then?" Her mother unraveled the scarf from around her neck and tucked it in her tote bag which she then hung on a little wooden knob in the shape of a star in the hallway.

"Nothing," Niamh said promptly. Morgan turned and gave her a look and Niamh's shoulders hunched a bit. "Ah, well, Mac asked me to go to the cove this morning and I ignored his messages."

"On purpose?" Morgan's voice went up a note in surprise.

"Aye, on purpose." Niamh dropped her head.

"Sure and that's not a nice thing to do for a friend, Niamh!" Morgan's voice was sharp. "Particularly when you're knowing what can happen at the cove. That's not safe…at all. What were you thinking?"

"That I wanted to not be distracted from my work and he's a grown man?" Niamh mumbled into her mug.

"Sure and that's fine if he's off for a walk in the park. But this is the cove, Niamh." Morgan pushed her sleeves up and washed her hands at the kitchen sink while continuing her lecture. "You know as well as anyone the dangers that can be found there. I'm right disappointed in you, I am."

"Didn't we tell him the other day not to go in the cove? He has all the information he needs, Mum." Niamh took a bite of her biscuit, furrowing her brow as she convinced herself that she'd done nothing wrong. "All three of us warned him away."

"Nevertheless, you know how stubborn men are."

Niamh huffed out a little laugh as she was looking at one of the most stubborn women in Ireland.

"I messaged Gracie to keep an eye out for him. She said she was home. I wasn't completely cold-hearted and sending him off to his death, you know."

"That's something then." Morgan turned, dish towel in hands, and studied her daughter. "When are you going to admit you have feelings for him?"

"I…" Niamh rolled her eyes. "He's just a friend. I told you that."

Morgan just waited patiently, not saying a word, and annoyance flashed through Niamh. She pushed away from the counter and began to pace.

"Methinks you protest too much," Morgan said.

"I don't know why everyone is so fixated on us getting together. Isn't it modern day now? Can't a woman and man be friends? He needed a friend…I am one to him. That's it."

"Yet you let him go into the cove on his own. Is that what a friend would do?"

"If that friend is busy…yes." Niamh pushed her lower lip out. "Again, must I remind you – we warned him."

"But you ignored his text. You didn't reply or reiterate to him that it was deeply unsafe to go there alone and then you took the coward's way out and had Gracie look after him."

Each word was like little poison darts hitting her skin and Niamh cringed.

"I'm an arse, aren't I?"

"Oh, Niamh." Morgan's face was wreathed in lines of sympathy. Coming forward, she put her arms around her daughter and pulled her into a hug. "He scares you, doesn't he?"

"Aye, he does," Niamh admitted, breathing in the scent of citrus that her mother loved to wear. It reminded her of sunny walks on a tropical island. "You're right. I didn't want to go with him to the cove. What if it glowed? What if he's…the one for me? How would I even begin to explain that? Or tell him, goddess forbid, who I actually am? Look at his life, Mum. Look at it! He's constantly under a lens. He's always being watched. There's no way that someone like me, who has to live her life with a particular level of privacy, could begin to manage. Don't you see?"

"So, it's his lifestyle that doesn't suit you – but not the man himself?" Niamh pulled away and met her mother's eyes.

It was a fair question and one that deeply rattled Niamh. She dropped to a chair at the table, taking a moment to consider the words. Whenever she was presented with a question in school, Niamh always tried to take her time to pick it up and analyze it from all sides. Now, she found that she'd deliberately been ignoring doing that when it came to Mac. Instead, she'd shoved him neatly in a cupboard in her mind, closing the door and throwing away the key.

"He's a good man," Niamh said carefully, shifting through her thoughts. "I think he's deeply lonely, and I know he has a difficult past. To the outside world, he looks like Mr. Popular, but I think he's searching for home. Everywhere he goes, he tries to create a sense of community – as though he can recreate the team experience. It's a safe space for him."

"That's the psychologist talking." Morgan tapped her hand to her heart. "What about Niamh?"

"I…I really like him." Niamh's words were but a whisper, the truth of them sending fear through her body like a cold gust of wind rolling down a wintry hill. "I think about him constantly. I can barely get work done. Thoughts of him intrude all day long. I love when he laughs…and how his smile and enthusiasm for life lights up a room. I love that he didn't blink when I told him what I was studying and instead helped me to get here and set up my lab. Many people have laughed at me for my work. He packed me up and drove me home and spent hours asking me about what I was learning. He cares about people, more so than I think anyone realizes. And I don't think he's remotely the playboy that the magazines paint him out to be. I think I let their image of him cloud my mind."

"How so?" Morgan took the seat across the table from Niamh.

"Because it's easier that way," Niamh said. "It's easier to believe the worst of him because then I don't have to look too deeply at my own feelings for him." And wasn't that delightful to have to admit to herself? It was annoying, really, that Niamh had reverted to classic protection measures. Keep Mac in the friend zone and she'd never get hurt, right? Because if she didn't try with him then she didn't have to ever find out if they weren't really suited for each other.

"Well, now. Isn't that something?" Morgan smiled gently at her. "You're a wonderful young woman, Niamh. And yet you've always kept men at a distance. I understand that – sure and I was the same myself, wasn't I? But look at the love that I did find when I gave myself permission to get out of my own way."

"What if...what if it all blows up in my face?" Niamh worried her bottom lip.

"And what if it's wonderful?"

"I'd really prefer to know the outcome now. You know...there is more than one of us who can take a peek into the future. Perhaps I should be having a chat with..."

"No." Morgan held up her hand. "No, Niamh. You

know as well as I do that those visions are susceptible to change. You have free will. You can always change the course of your future. Don't you understand? There are no guarantees in life. Even if you get a reading that shows you and Mac happily-ever-after…then what? Then you'd be willing to take the risk?"

"I think it would help, yeah," Niamh said. She ran a hand over her face. "It would be comforting, I guess."

"I hadn't realized that I raised such a fearful daughter." Morgan's words might as well have been a slap.

"I…I'm not!" Niamh pushed back from the table. "It's just…it's a big deal, Mum."

"You said as much, earlier, didn't you then? You said he scares you." Morgan pressed on. "And what's on the other side of fear?"

"Opportunity," Niamh said, automatically. Morgan had drilled the concept into her from a young age.

"Your man's here. What's it going to be?" Morgan said, a few seconds before a knock sounded at the door.

Panic skittered through Niamh as she looked down at her comfy clothes. She hadn't even showered yet today.

"Can you?" Niamh motioned to the door, not asking how Morgan knew who it was.

"Nope." Morgan said, studying a chip in her nail polish.

"Well, sure and you're annoying aren't you then?" Heat flamed in Niamh's cheeks as she all but stomped to the front door. Pulling it open, she saw Mac standing there with a smile on his face and flowers in his arms.

"Delivery for you," Mac said, handing her the bunch of flowers, and Niamh's heart flipped. She stepped back, burying her face in the blooms, and Mac's presence filled the room as he came inside. He was just so…everything, Niamh thought, his very energy seeming to reach out to meld with hers.

"These are lovely, thank you," Niamh said. "Ah, I'm sorry about not returning your text earlier. I was in the lab and…well." Niamh didn't want to say anymore because she didn't want to outright lie to Mac. He didn't deserve that from her.

"It's fine. The cove was grand," Mac said, but there was a flash in his eyes that made Niamh desperately curious.

"Did you go to the cove, Mac?" Morgan said, from the doorway, concern on her lovely face. "Not in it, I hope?"

"Sure and I went. I can see why it's such a magnificent spot."

Niamh shot a quick look at Morgan while they both tried to determine if he'd actually gone in the cove or stood on the cliffs overlooking it. Niamh opened her mouth to ask, but Mac cut her off.

"I stopped by to ask you if you'll have dinner with me." A hopeful look bloomed on Mac's face, causing Niamh's body to go on alert. Yes, oh yes, she wanted to have dinner and so much more with this man.

"Um, well." Worry crept in and Niamh stiffened when Morgan cleared her throat behind her. "Yes, thank you. That would be nice, I'm sure. When?"

"Now?" Mac asked, a smile blooming on his face as Niamh looked askance down at her outfit.

"I haven't even showered today. No, not now."

"Okay, in fifteen minutes then?" Mac glanced at the iWatch on his wrist.

It was just Mac, Niamh reminded herself. She didn't need to get fancy for him or anything like that. He'd asked her to dinner, but hadn't specified if this was a date.

"Why don't you come in Mac, while Niamh takes a quick shower?" Morgan suggested and Mac grinned, knowing full well that Niamh didn't want him to come inside.

Feeling a bit steamrolled, Niamh gestured for Mac to come further inside and then handed her flowers to her mother as she passed her.

"Can you put these in water please while I shower?"

CHAPTER 20

*N*iamh didn't have much time to overthink what she was going to wear – in fact she didn't even know where they were going – but it was cold out and most restaurants in Grace's Cove were fairly casual – so she pulled on dark jeans, a crushed velvet cowl-necked top in a deep purple color and clipped her hair back with a sparkly comb. Vanity won out and she took a few moments to cover the dark circles under her eyes and apply just a touch of makeup so that overall she looked refreshed. Grabbing her leather jacket and purse, Niamh went to the kitchen where Mac chatted easily with her mother at the kitchen table. He looked so large there, next to Morgan, and Niamh was struck once again by how his presence seemed to fill a room. She wondered if other people saw him the same way or if it was just her?

"You look nice," Mac said. His face lit when he saw her, and Niamh felt his words warm her. Her mind flashed back to the models from the night before. They'd been dressed much fancier than she was, and doubt filled her as she glanced down at her outfit. Perhaps she should have taken more time with her look. Didn't she have tons of cool clothes from vintage stores all over Dublin? Maybe she should have chosen something with more personality.

"You do," Morgan agreed. "I love that velvet top. What a great fabric…it just makes you want to touch it, doesn't it then?" Morgan reached out and stroked a hand down Niamh's arm while Niamh almost choked at the image that her mother's words brought to her mind. Shooting a quick glance at Mac, she saw his grin widen.

"I'm not sure how to politely answer that," Mac finally said, and Niamh's humiliation was complete.

"Oh! Aren't you the cheeky one?" Morgan laughed, a loud and boisterous sound, and swatted him on the arm. "Go on then, have fun you two. I'll just see to putting dinner on for that wayward father of yours."

"Wayward is hardly the word I'd use for him. He's blind for you," Niamh pointed out as she slid her arms into her coat.

"And well he should be. I'm fabulous, aren't I?" Morgan fluttered her lashes at Niamh.

"He's a lucky man," Mac agreed and taking Niamh's arm, he drew her outside into the pelting rain. "Hurry now."

"Oh, I didn't bring…" Niamh stopped when she saw his SUV in the drive and sprinted for it. Jumping in the passenger side, she wiped the rain from her face and immediately wondered if her makeup had held up.

"I'm glad I drove," Mac laughed, also wiping the rain from his face. "I should've grabbed an umbrella, but I was out all day."

Guilt shot through Niamh, and she wondered again if he'd tried to go into the cove. Perhaps not. The man seemed to be good at taking instructions, and Gracie's text message had said he was fine. She was likely overthinking things.

"It's Ireland. I should be prepared for constantly changing weather," Niamh laughed. "Where are we going for dinner? I have to admit, I'm famished. I only had the biscuit with my tea just now. It's been a busy day." *Of trying to focus on my work and not think about you,* Niamh silently added.

"Oh well, it's nothing fancy," Mac said. He drove up the main road of Grace's Cove and toward his rental house.

"Are we going to your place?" He hadn't invited her over, and though Niamh had been curious to see how he was living in his rental space, she'd held back from asking to see it.

"Yes, I'm going to give cooking a go," Mac said with a resolute tone.

"Is that right?" A little shiver of anticipation worked its way through Niamh as she realized that this might actually be a date. A man didn't bring a woman home and cook for her if they were just friends. Or was she just hyping things up in her head?

"I can't promise it will be edible. But I'm sticking to an easy recipe, and I think we'll be okay. Alright then, we're here." Mac glanced out of the window. The last dredges of the day's light clung to the murky sky and rain pounded the roof. "Shall we wait a moment?"

"Knowing Ireland this could be a minute or hours. I

say let's go for it," Niamh said. Because if she sat cocooned in this car with the rain falling around them, Niamh might just do something silly like lean over and kiss Mac. His closeness was overwhelming, and Niamh went a bit heady at the thought of kissing him again.

"Race ya." Mac dashed from the car with Niamh following suit, giggling as icy rain slapped her in the face, cooling the heat of her cheeks. By the time they tumbled in through the front door, laughing and gasping, Niamh was well soaked.

"I suppose I could have held off on the shower if I knew I was going to be getting one," Niamh laughed.

"Och, that was worse than I thought it would be." Rain dripped down Mac's shoulders and landed with little plops on the floor. "Let me get you some towels. Um…do you want something else to wear? You're soaked through."

Niamh glanced down to see her leather coat open and the velvet shirt molded to her. The velvet that her mother had so loudly proclaimed was delightful to touch looked almost sinful across her breasts. If she was another woman, in another time – a courtesan perhaps – Niamh would have peeled the leather jacket off and sent Mac a come-hither look. Instead she just gulped and nodded as the heat of nervousness flashed across her skin.

"Be right back then." Mac dashed off down the hallway and Niamh took the time to look at the room. The main door opened directly into the living area where large picture windows showcased a lovely view of, well, right now the pouring rain. Mac had pulled the couch to the side of the room, creating a more open space where he'd laid out a variety of exercise equipment like weights and mats.

Had he brought all of that with him? Niamh wondered if he traveled like that often. It must just be part of the job, staying in amazing shape, and Niamh's mouth went dry imagining him here each morning, in just a pair of shorts, lifting weights while sweat glistened on his muscles.

"Niamh?"

"Oh!" Niamh jumped, pulling her mind away from those images, and gratefully accepted the towel he handed her.

"I also brought you something to change into if you didn't want to sit around in wet clothes."

Niamh thought of her shirt.

"Yes, that's great. Thanks." Accepting the bundle of clothes from him, she followed his directions to the bathroom and closed the door behind her. Blowing out a breath, she caught sight of her reflection in the mirror and winced. *Of course* she'd had to go and put makeup on. Dark streaks rimmed her eyes where her mascara had smudged in the rain, making her look like a drowned raccoon. With a sigh, Niamh grabbed some toilet paper and set to cleaning her face up. Once presentable, she pulled her shirt and jeans off, but left her underwear on.

"Well then." Niamh held up the long-sleeved jersey he'd brought for her to wear. Two of her could easily have fit inside it. But, at the very least, she wasn't going to look like walking sex, so that was something. Niamh tugged it over her head and giggled when the hem hit her mid-thigh. Next, she pulled on the sweatpants he'd given her, rolling the waist band several times until they were comfortable. Nope, nothing sexy about this get-up, Niamh decided, but was happy to be warm and dry. Despite herself, Niamh took a little sniff of the shirt she'd pulled on, and a hint of Mac's aftershave wafted to her. Her stomach twisted in knots. This felt almost too cozy, like something a girlfriend would do, and Niamh had to forcibly remind herself that they, above anything else, had agreed to be friends. Friends gave each other dry clothes. Simple as that.

Friends didn't bring you flowers and cook for you. Niamh shoved that thought aside and left the bathroom to join Mac in the kitchen. He'd changed as well and wore comfy grey sweatpants and a deep blue long-sleeved Henley that made his eyes pop.

"Ah, and now that's a pretty sight." Mac beamed. "Sure and you looked lovely before, but there's nothing like a beautiful woman wearing your jersey."

"Oh is this yours? I hadn't noticed," Niamh teased. She'd noticed. She'd even twisted around in the mirror to see his name across her back.

"Shots fired." Mac held a hand to his chest as though he'd been wounded. "Either way, I like how it looks on you Niamh. You should keep it."

"What? I can't keep your jersey," Niamh exclaimed. *Keep it*, her mind told her. *Keep it and sleep in it and dream about all the what-ifs.*

"Sure you can. I have loads."

"Ah, you give them away to all the girls then." Niamh kept her tone playful though she really wanted to know.

"Nope, never have before. Wine's breathing on the table if you want a glass." Mac turned his attention back to the stove where several pans sat on the burners.

"Do you want a glass of wine?" Niamh asked, pleased to know she was the first to have a MacGregor jersey from the man himself. Even if he wasn't telling her the truth, it still made her feel good. Settling into a dining chair, she poured herself a glass of the red wine.

"I'm good. I've got a beer here." Mac pointed to a bottle of Smithwick's on the counter.

"This is a nice kitchen." Niamh took in the sleek cabinets, simple white marble countertops, and another picture window looking out to the hills. "It's more modern than I was expecting it to be."

"It is at that. I like that they kind of kept comfort and charm in the living room and bedrooms but updated the kitchen. I bet this place is booked out all summer."

"Likely so. They do a good business with their rentals. Grace's Cove is a really popular destination in the summer. Particularly with Americans who love to take photographs and get a proper Irish pub experience. Plus, there's loads of good hikes through the hills. You can have an hour walk or a day's long walk and always see something lovely." Niamh was about to ask him what he'd seen at the cove that day when he swore loudly at the stove.

"Shite! Stupid pan…" Mac grabbed the smoking pan and dumped it in the sink, running cold water over the entire thing, a cloud of smoke rising from the pan. An acrid smell filled the room and Mac crossed to the window and opened it, a cool breeze instantly sweeping through the room.

"Um." Niamh took in the frustrated look on Mac's face. "Do you want to tell me what happened?"

"Stupid pan. Stupid cooking." Mac muttered, staring down at the sink.

Niamh crossed the kitchen and looked down at the

mess in the pan. It appeared to be very badly burned chicken.

"Tell me what you did? Or at the very least what you were trying to make?"

"I was going to try Chicken Alfredo. Just something easy I thought. And I know you need to cook the chicken well and…" Mac gestured with the beer in his hand. "Here we are."

"But what *exactly* did you do?"

"I put the chicken in the pan. I turned the stove on. That's as far as I got." Mac shook his head sadly at the mess.

"No oil?" Niamh's eyebrows rose when Mac looked at her in question. "No butter? No water?"

"Um…no?"

"Oh, right. Got it. You really don't know how to cook do you?" Niamh immediately felt bad when an embarrassed look flashed over his face. This was a man used to doing things well, Niamh reminded herself. "Hey, it's not a big deal. I've made the same mistake before, too. We all learn at some point. But you can't just put raw chicken in a pan with nothing to lubricate it. It will stick and burn."

"Oh. Like this."

"Right, just like this. But that's okay, really. Mac, it was very sweet of you to try something new for me. I appreciate it."

"I thought I knew how to cook. I fended for myself a lot as…" Mac's words trailed off and he shook his head. "I can't believe I screwed this up. I was going to wow you with my prowess in the kitchen. Then maybe sweet talk you into another kiss."

There it was, Niamh thought, as lightness spread through her. Confirmation that this was more than friends and he was still interested in her, no matter how many times she'd pushed him to the friend zone.

"Well, a valiant effort like this certainly deserves a kiss," Niamh said. She stood up on her tiptoes and brushed a kiss across his cheek. She couldn't quite work up her courage to kiss him on the lips. Stepping back before the moment could evolve into something Niamh wasn't sure she was ready for, she smiled brightly up at him. "Why don't I just take a peek at what else you have here? Or we can order in."

"There's frozen pizza," Mac said. His look was heavy with lust and something more, and Niamh felt herself caught in it for a moment.

"Right. Pizza is perfect. I love pizza. I live for pizza. Shall we do that then?" Niamh crossed to the freezer and laughed when she saw a stack of pizza boxes. "I see this is a fan favorite."

"You can't go wrong with pizza. That I *have* mastered." Mac's voice was teasing once again, and the moment passed. "Move aside, lovely lady, and let me impress you with my unboxing skills."

Niamh laughed and settled back into her seat at the table though her mind whirled at the potential for what could happen this evening. Would he kiss her again? She found that she wanted him to, very much so. And yet, Niamh still held herself a bit back from him. What was it about Mac that worried her so? Her wall was still up with him, and Niamh wondered if she was being entirely unfair.

Mac whirled suddenly, a knife in hand, and Niamh's eyes widened.

"Oh my."

Mac held the box up and neatly sliced the cardboard open with a dramatic flair and slid the pre-packaged pizza from the carton. With another twirl, he dipped low with the pizza held high over his head and then sliced neatly through the plastic and placed the pizza on the tray on the counter. After putting it in the oven, he set a timer and turned to her.

"Ta-da. Dinner will be ready shortly."

"Well done, good sir. Bravo!" Niamh brought her fingers to her lips and made a kissing noise and Mac bowed.

"Shall we go to the couch? These chairs are not that comfortable," Mac said. He topped off her wine and opened another beer for himself. Niamh glanced at the thin wooden dining chairs and realized they likely were a pain for a man of Mac's size.

"Sure, let's."

Mac stopped by the small fireplace in the living room and in a matter of moments cheerful flames flickered there, adding a nice ambience to the room. He might be bad at cooking, but the man was great with fires, Niamh decided.

"That was quick."

"I like having a fire. We didn't have a fireplace growing up. Now I always want one. I used to go to friends' houses and it always seemed so cozy in the winter to gather around the fire." Mac shrugged one shoulder as he studied the flames for a moment. Once he was certain the fire would stay lit, he crossed the room and joined Niamh on the deep-seated leather couch. The rain continued to pound outside and a howl of wind buffeted the cottage.

"What were winters like for you then?" Niamh already knew he'd had a tough upbringing, though he hadn't expanded on it much.

"I'd sit on the floor near the radiator to get as much warmth as I could while I studied rugby plays and waited for my soup to heat up."

"Oh. Your dad didn't cook for you?"

"The only time I got a fresh meal was if I made it or my dad brought a new woman home." Mac laughed and looked away, a derisive look on his face. "Not that he brought women home all that often. Even they could see what a loser he was."

"I'm sorry to hear that, Mac." Niamh's heart went out to him. She'd been lucky enough to grow up in a loving home, but her mother had been an orphan who'd gone through traumatic experiences. At the very least, she could empathize with him.

"And yet I still get him tickets to every game." The note of yearning in his voice pierced Niamh's core. She scooted closer to him on the couch so she leaned against him, sensing he couldn't look her in the eyes right now.

"Does he come and watch?"

"He scalps them. For money to take to the bookies." Mac's voice was tense.

"Well, that's just plain shite." Niamh sat up, outraged. "You need to stop leaving tickets for him."

"It is what it is." Mac shrugged one shoulder and Niamh reached out, placing her hand on his arm.

"Mac. Listen to me. You owe him nothing. Nothing at all, do you hear me? Don't keep giving him tickets if this is what he does. You deserve to be surrounded by people who support you."

"Ah, it's nothing." Mac waved it away.

"It's not nothing." Niamh insisted. "You have the power now, Mac. You aren't a child anymore. He doesn't get to dictate your life. I give you full permission to stop catering to a man that doesn't show up for you."

"It's not his fault," Mac said, refusing to meet her eyes.

"What? Sure and you have to be out of your mind. Of course it's his fault. He was the adult. You were the child. His job was to take care of you and clearly he didn't. Why do you need to be taking care of him now?"

"Because if I don't…he'll tell the world what I am."

CHAPTER 21

*H*is words hung heavy in the air between them and Niamh's brain scrambled to make sense of them.

"And what are you, Mac? A child who needed love? A man with a good heart? An excellent rugby player? A great friend?" Niamh asked, carefully picking her way through what felt like a field full of landmines.

"No, Niamh." Mac turned to her and his eyes were stormy with emotion. "I'm something more."

An awareness rippled through Niamh, and she narrowed her eyes at him as her thoughts bounced back to Gracie's text earlier that day. She'd said Mac had been fine. Had he gone to the cove and not gotten hurt? Was he…?

"Mac. Did you go into the cove today?" Niamh kept her voice steady, but her pulse raced.

"I did."

"Did…did anything happen to you there?" Niamh's voice dropped to almost a whisper.

"I wasn't injured if that's what you're meaning."

"So you did the little ritual before stepping onto the beach?" Surely someone at the pub had told him a safe way to enter the cove. That was likely it.

"No, Niamh. Nobody told me about any ritual."

"What…what happened while you were there?"

"I'm guessing you know a woman named Fiona?" Mac's eyes were on hers, and Niamh took a large gulp of her wine.

"She showed herself to you?"

"Ah, so you'll admit there's ghosts."

"Of course I'll admit that." Niamh laughed, despite the seriousness of the conversation. "Mac, I study all sorts of things outside what a lot of people allow themselves to believe. Not to mention that Fiona is kin to me of sorts and I see her occasionally as well."

"She's a nice woman. Commanding," Mac said, a thoughtful expression on his face.

"She is at that. Fiona was…well, still is…a powerhouse."

"Gracie came down to the beach as well. Apparently her dog warned her that I was going to the beach."

"Rosie." Niamh nodded. "She's a good dog."

"Gracie's a good person as well. She dropped what she was doing to make sure that I hadn't been harmed. That's a long hike down the cliffs to check on someone she barely knows."

"She has a good heart, Gracie. She's a healer as well." Niamh didn't elaborate on what type of healer. "It's in her nature to take care of people."

"Both Fiona and Gracie seemed overly surprised that I

was on the beach. Even more that I wasn't broken and bleeding," Mac continued, his voice steady, though his eyes grew stormy with each passing moment. He pulled a small couch cushion onto his lap, hugging it in front of him as though for protection.

"It's said that the beach recognizes her own. But even then the waters there can be…finicky." Niamh picked her words carefully as realization began to work its way through her. If Mac could go on the beach, well, then he was likely of Grace O'Malley's bloodline. Which meant…

"Right. So I'm told." Mac took a long sip of his beer.

"Mac. Mac, look at me." Niamh tugged at his arm, forcing his eyes back to her. "Do you have an extrasensory ability? Is that what you're working yourself up to tell me? Because you have to know this is a very safe space, right?"

"I know." Mac's voice was haunting in its nervousness.

Niamh let the silence draw out between them, not wanting to push him, and also not wanting to lead him. She almost toppled off the couch when the timer sounded for the pizza.

"I'll just…" Mac hopped up and went into the kitchen to pull the pizza from the oven. Niamh waited, her mind racing through a million questions. Did Mac have powers? Did this mean they were related in some distant way? If so…what would that mean? She would have to cut off any feelings she was entertaining for him.

"Are you good with eating on the couch?" Mac came back in the room with two plates and the wine bottle tucked under his arm. Niamh wasn't sure how she was even going to eat like this, not when he'd left her hanging in the middle of such crucial information.

"Sure, that's fine." Niamh took the plate and put it aside, barely glancing at the pizza.

"Top off?" Mac motioned to her glass which Niamh was surprised to see was empty.

"Sure." Niamh waited while he filled her glass, waited while he sat down, waited while he took a bite of pizza. Finally, when she was about to explode from nerves, he looked up at her.

"Not hungry?"

"Mac." Niamh just leveled a look at him and he sighed before putting the slice of pizza back on his plate.

"I would prefer if we didn't make this a huge deal. So, you know, go on and eat your pizza. It makes me uncomfortable when you stare me down like I'm one of your patients or something. I don't...I'm not used to..." Mac huffed out an annoyed breath. "This isn't easy for me."

"Oh. Of course, right." Niamh shook her head to clear her mind. She'd learned about this in her courses in school. She was letting her own personal interests get invested in the process, making him feel uncomfortable. "Pizza looks great. Not a single burn mark to be seen anywhere."

"I told you, didn't I? I'm the master."

"You did. Hey, Mac. Thanks for dinner." She held up her glass and tapped it to his bottle in a silent cheers before taking a bite of the pizza. They fell into a companionable silence for a moment as they both ate. "That hits the spot. Pizza is a favorite of mine, but don't be telling my mother that."

"I promise." Mac had finished four slices to her one already. Niamh put her plate aside for a moment, letting her food settle, and took another sip of her wine. The night had taken on a warm fuzzy glow, likely helped by the two glasses of wine, and she settled more deeply into the couch. Mac stood and crossed the room, poking at the fire and adding a few more logs before casually looking over his shoulder.

"I do have abilities. I can sense things a few moments before they happen."

Niamh froze, her eyes on Mac's back as he continued to poke at the fire, likely for something to do with his hands because it was already blazing merrily along. A light roll of thunder sounded in the distance and the intensity of the rain increased.

"That's certainly an interesting ability to have. Are you willing to share a little more with me...for example how that manifests exactly for you?" Niamh tried to keep her voice as neutral as possible.

Mac turned, his eyebrows raised to his hairline, and just looked at her.

"What?" Niamh asked.

"Listen, Niamh. If I'm going to talk about this...I'd really appreciate it if you didn't use your doctor voice like I was someone to be analyzed. Just talk to me in your normal voice like a friend would."

"Oh." Niamh deflated. "I was trying to sound as open and encouraging as I could."

"You sounded clinical."

"Okay, well, for fuck's sake then," Niamh said with a laugh. "Sure and that's an incredible ability to have. Tell me everything about it. Like...if I were to throw..." Niamh looked around and chucked a couch cushion at him but his hands were already in the air ready to catch it.

"Yeah, something like that." Mac grinned. "And, much better. I prefer this Niamh."

"Oh, sure and that's cool. You don't like it when I use everything I've learned in school to speak to you, but if I curse and throw a pillow at your head, it's all good?"

"Pretty much." Mac slowly advanced toward her.

"But…so. How? Because I'm wondering where you get this from. Some of it is just how it is. Some of these powers are passed down magickly through bloodlines." Niamh's pulse kicked up as Mac continued his advance and leaned over her. Bracketing his arms on both sides of her, he stopped.

"Fiona and Gracie seem to think it is from a daughter that a man name Dillon didn't know about."

"Oh…" The thought had never occurred to her that the great Grace O'Malley would have extended her enchantment to include other people she cared for. "So we're not related."

"Was that your biggest concern?" A predatory look came into Mac's eyes. "That we might be related?"

"I mean, yes, it popped into my head. Very briefly, of course." Niamh's pulse kicked up, and her stomach did a funny little twist as Mac's eyes dipped to her lips and then trailed down her body.

"And it doesn't bother you…that I have abilities? Or powers as you call them? Because if you were more worried about us being related, then I'm thinking your mind might have been on other things…" Mac's voice dropped lower, his lips hovering inches from hers now, and Niamh lost herself for a moment in his eyes.

"Powers?" Niamh asked, her mind blurred and Mac laughed.

"Niamh."

"Yes?"

"Do you want me to kiss you?"

"Oh…" Niamh breathed, trying to break the spell his mere presence weaved around her. "Yes, well, I think that I do."

"To be clear…" Mac leaned forward and brushed his lips ever so softly across hers. "You are the only person other than my father that I have openly told about my extrasensory powers. Abilities. Gifts. Curse. Whatever you want to call it. I'm trusting you…well, because Gracie said I should. That I needed to be open with you if I wanted this to go anywhere." Once more he dipped his mouth to hers for a taste.

"Wait, you talked to Gracie about this before me? She knows you have powers?" Distracted, Niamh pulled back and put her hand on his chest.

"She found me in the cove unharmed talking to a ghost. She had a few questions."

"Right. Um, okay. Right. So, to answer your question – no it doesn't bother me in the slightest. I think it's fascinating. And I appreciate you sharing this information with me." Niamh put her finger to Mac's lips when he tried to lean in again. "While my integrity is impeccable as a friend, I will also tell you that I can extend my professional courtesy to you as well, Mac. Your secret will always be safe with me."

"Niamh," Mac's voice was but a whisper at her lips. "I ache for you."

"Oh…" Niamh breathed. "I thought…I…"

"You have to know I'm in Grace's Cove for you, Niamh."

"But you needed to get away…" Niamh blinked up at him.

"Niamh. I can go anywhere in the world. Anytime I want. I have friends with private islands. I can go as remote as I want to and disappear as much as I need to. Did you really think that little Grace's Cove would be an actual hideout spot?"

"I guess I didn't think it…" Gracie's words flitted back to her. A man doesn't pack up and drive across the country with a woman if he just wants to be friends.

"I'm trying to be patient with you. I'm giving you space. I'm not dating your friends. I've bared my soul to you with my deepest secret. If you don't like me, Niamh, tell me now because there's nothing else that I can do to show you who I am as a person. I will respect your decision, but I need you to be honest with me. Because even though you told me you just wanted to be friends when we met, I really feel like there is more here. If there's not… then you have my heartfelt apologies for misreading this situation and I hope you don't hate me for pressing the issue with you. I guess I just had to try once more to see if you would give me a chance once you knew me better as a person."

Niamh's heart all but came to a stand-still as this gorgeous man hovered over her on the couch, his eyes warm with emotion, his heart on his sleeve. A sliver of trepidation worked through her because she knew it would be difficult to be his girlfriend – to date in the public eye.

But would it be worth it? If it meant she got to be with him? It felt a bit like stepping off a ledge into the unknown. Niamh realized just how vulnerable Mac had made himself for her. His whole life he'd sheltered a secret that he'd only now shared with one person. Her. Men didn't do those kinds of things if they didn't value you, Niamh told herself.

"I like you, Mac. A lot, actually. I've been trying to think of you as just a friend, but..." Niamh smiled a sheepish smile up at him. "It's not working. No matter how much I try. I want...I want more, Mac...I want you."

"Well, now, then I'll just have to give you that, won't I?" Mac's voice held a dangerous note that made Niamh shiver in anticipation. Suddenly desperate, he attacked her soft lips, sucking on the bottom one until it swelled. Dropping to his knees in front of her, Mac shifted Niamh, arranging her body as though she was a doll, and moved himself between her legs. He continued his assault on her mouth, his relentless pursuit and intense focus shooting lust straight through her entire body. Niamh gasped against his lips, shocked at the emotions that washed through her. She'd never felt this way for someone before.

Mac paused his kisses, leaning back to run his hands over her arms, down her sides, and to her legs. For a moment, he knelt before her, a gilded fallen angel – all muscles and depravity – before reaching for her socks. Niamh laughed a little as he pulled each sock off, and the cool air hit her toes. Gently, Mac traced his fingers over her ankles before sliding his hands beneath the sweatpants to massage her calves.

"I want to take these off. I want to look at you.

Gorgeous Niamh. The girl next door with the stunning brain. Will you show yourself to me?" Mac asked as he continued to run his hands further up her legs until he reached the soft skin of her thighs. Niamh wasn't sure she was capable of words so she merely lifted one of her legs and Mac laughed. Capturing her lips once more, he stood and lifted Niamh as if she weighed nothing at all and slid both her sweatpants and her underpants down her legs before plopping her back down. Niamh squeaked as the cool leather hit her bare legs. She hadn't expected him to also take her underwear and now she felt exposed, sitting there, legs sprawled open, wearing only his jersey. She felt vulnerable…and fiercely turned on. Niamh wanted him to claim her as his.

"You're incredible." Mac's voice was hoarse, and his breath had picked up as though he'd run several miles. "A dream, Niamh. You are a dream come true." His words resonated through her, and Niamh squirmed on the couch, wanting him closer…wanting everything with him. When his lips brushed the skin of her inner thigh, she jumped, and a giggle escaped her.

"Ticklish?" Mac asked, leaning back to look up at her.

"Oh just…nervous. Excited." Niamh immediately corrected when she saw the concern flash through his eyes.

"I'll take it nice and slow, Niamh."

"Oh, but I wish you wouldn't." Niamh shocked them both by saying. She slapped a hand over her mouth as she couldn't believe those words had just tumbled out of her. But, truth be told, she was all but writhing with need and the man had barely touched her.

"Is that right? The lady likes it fast?" Mac shocked her

by dipping his head to her center and sucking, sending a sharp spear of lust through her and causing her to arch off the couch in desire. Pleasure rocked through her and Niamh bucked against him once more as he slid a finger inside her, testing her.

"Mac...please..." Niamh's cries turned into a soft keening note as he plunged her neatly over the edge into a silvery pool of lust.

"Niamh. Hold on. Just hold." Mac shot up and ran into his bedroom before racing back into the living room, condom in hand. Niamh gaped as he stripped, goggling at the sheer mass of him – everywhere – and blinked at him when he knelt once more and then roundly cursed.

"What's wrong?" Niamh felt almost drugged, so loose she was with the little shivers of pleasure that still rocketed through her.

"Never mind it. Niamh, look at me." Mac traced the edge of the jersey, before slipping his hands beneath. Gently, his hands trailed across the soft skin of her stomach before cupping her breasts. Niamh bowed, throwing her head back, offering herself to his careful administrations as he teased her mercilessly. Brushing his hard length against her, Mac bent and licked at her neck, blowing a soft breath of air against her sensitive skin. Niamh, desperate for him, shoved her hips forward, trying to take what she wanted so very much.

"Niamh. Look at me."

Niamh met his eyes and saw a thousand truths there.

"You matter. More than anyone else in my life. I'm sorry our first time is on a couch in the living room, but I don't think I've ever wanted someone as much as I do you…ever." Mac's voice came out in tight little bursts, as though the strain of holding himself back from her was killing him.

"Please, Mac. I want you, too. So, *so* much." Niamh cried out when he entered her in one long thrust and then they were lost to each other, the rain pounding outside, the light of the fire flickering gently across them as they made promises to each other over and over until they both shivered with release.

Once finished, Mac just held her against him, schooling his breathing and Niamh tried to process all of her emotions. One thing stood out to her.

"What were you swearing about?" Niamh tilted her head up to look at Mac and a grin flashed in his handsome face.

"I knelt in the pizza."

Laughter ripped through Niamh and she leaned carefully forward to see Mac kneeling on her forgotten plate of pizza.

"And you didn't move?" Niamh raised an eyebrow at him.

"And miss out on you demanding me to hurry? Not in this lifetime, love. But, for the record? The second time's going to be much slower."

Niamh squealed with laughter as he picked her up and carried her to the bedroom.

CHAPTER 22

*T*he week flew by in a blur for Niamh as she struggled to focus on her studies while not getting lost in silly daydreams of Mac. Her parents hadn't asked once about her not coming home most evenings, and she'd spent more than one overnight at Mac's rental cottage. Not every night, as Niamh was still nervous about moving too fast with him, but the more time she spent with Mac, the more she understood what a miracle it was that he had evolved into the kind-hearted and genuine person that he was today.

"Oh, you've got it bad." Gracie's voice startled her from her thoughts and she blinked to where Kira and Gracie were grinning at her across the long wooden kitchen table in Gracie's cottage. Though Gracie and her husband Dylan could have afforded to own a mansion, Gracie's stubbornness had won out and they lived together in the little cottage tucked by the cliffs of the cove. Dylan supplemented his need for more space by dragging Gracie from the cottage on occasional trips to exotic places, and from what Niamh could see, they were blissfully happy.

"Lay off the poor girl, or you'll scare her away," Dylan said from where he sat in a wooden rocking chair by the little fire in the corner and consulted his iPad. "You're too pushy."

"Oh, pushy is it now? Well, I'm happy for you to push your way right on out of girls' night. You're ruining the energy in here with your useless comments," Gracie shot back.

When they weren't fighting, that was. Niamh was certain they considered fighting foreplay, because the sparks that bounced between the two when Dylan shot Gracie a look was enough to heat the whole room.

"I was just on my way out, my dearest love. I'm meeting Liam and Brogan over at the nature center. We're going to have a pint."

"At the nature center? In the dead of winter?"

"Sure and it's a grand spot. They've got the café set up and…well, why not?"

"Go on then. No need for you to keep blathering on." Gracie grinned widely when Dylan dropped a kiss on her mouth and then muttered something in her ear before saying his goodbye to the ladies.

"There, now. A proper girls' night," Gracie said and held up her wine glass. The three women clinked glasses and then looked down at the table where Gracie had laid out a row of jars.

"If it's a girls' night – why are we working? For you? This feels like unpaid labor," Kira griped.

"Oh hush. It's just potting up a few creams and tonics. Surely you won't be working up a sweat over such difficult labor now?" Gracie rolled her eyes. Her mass of hair was braided back from her face in an intricate knot, and she wore a leather apron tied loosely over her jumper.

"I don't mind it. These smell heavenly." Niamh sniffed one of the creams and sighed happily at the fresh sea salt scent.

"See? Some of us can take pleasure in the little things." Gracie glared to Kira who just grinned.

"How is the nature center doing?" Niamh asked, diverting the conversation away from her and Mac as she spooned some cream into a jar. "I imagine it's slow in winter?"

"Brogan's loving it. You should see how lit up he gets at creating new displays and adding new elements. There's always something to be done, to be fixed or updated, and he really couldn't be happier. And, even though it is winter, we're finding that if we host some classes, people are willing to come out and make a day of it. I've led some photography classes that have had a good turnout. We've had a few people speak about birdwatching and stuff like that. Birders…wow, what a group." Kira laughed and shook her head. "I had no idea what a huge community they are. But they're obsessed! And, I have to admit – my bird photography sells very well. Even I'm getting a little caught up in it."

"Birds are awesome," Gracie said with a little shrug, "but I still love Fergal the best."

"Is he okay in the winter?" Niamh looked up in concern. Fergal the otter had become famous with Kira's fun Instagram photos of him and his little otter family. The account had helped to drive traffic to the nature center, and now Fergal had become the official mascot of the center.

"Oh sure and he's grand. They're keeping warm enough."

"That's good to hear. They're right darling aren't they? I just…" Niamh glanced up to see both the women staring at her. She looked down and saw that she had overflowed the jar with cream and it was dripping over the side. "Oh! Gracie! I'm so sorry. I didn't mean to waste…I'll pay you for it, of course."

"Oh hush, I can make a batch of this in a small matter of time. But enough about otters, Niamh. Talk to us." Gracie handed her a towel.

Niamh blew out a breath as she schooled her thoughts. She had to be careful how she spoke about Mac because Kira didn't know his secret.

"How did you feel when he told you about his powers?" Kira asked and Niamh dropped the towel and shot Gracie a furious look.

"How could you?" Niamh whispered.

"I didn't!" Gracie held her hand to her heart. "I swear to Fiona, I did not."

"But how…" Niamh looked at Kira, worry racing through her that Mac's secret was already slipping away from her.

"Rosie." Kira shrugged and nodded to the dog who slumbered on her bed by the fire. Hearing her name, she got up and padded over to the table to tilt her head curiously at the group. "She's hoping for a treat."

One of Kira's strongest extrasensory abilities was to

communicate with animals, something which had paired perfectly with Brogan's love of nature and the nature center. Niamh had always admired the trait, because who wouldn't want to get an idea of what animals had to say? It was like adding extra layers of intrigue to your friend group. But now? With secrets being told? Niamh wasn't happy. She looked down at Rosie.

"That's not being a good dog, Rosie. You can't share secrets," Niamh chided the dog gently. Rosie turned her head to lift her sweet brown eyes to Niamh's for a long moment before plopping to the ground and burying her snout beneath her paws as though to cover her eyes in embarrassment. Immediately, guilt ran through Niamh.

"She is telling me she didn't know it was a secret. Rosie just thought it was fun that she had more people to play with on the beach," Kira said, translating the dogs thoughts for the women.

Instantly contrite, Niamh dropped to the floor and gave Rosie a hug.

"I'm sorry, I shouldn't have scolded you. Of course you don't understand why it would be a secret." Rosie gave Niamh's face a sloppy lick and Niamh laughed, rubbing the back of her hand across her cheek and then just sat there, cuddling the dog for a bit.

"If it helps…I don't know what his powers are. Just that he has them and that he can go in the cove. Much to the surprise of everyone, it seems." Kira shrugged.

"So, this is actually a huge deal for him. You *really* can't tell anyone. You either, Gracie. I'm assuming you didn't tell, Dylan, correct? Or did you do the married person thing where you tell all the secrets?"

"In this case, I did not say anything to Dylan as Mac had asked me, very nicely, to respect his privacy. I know as much as anyone what having extra abilities can do to a person's reputation," Gracie said.

"I'm the only person that he's openly told…at least that's what he said," Niamh said. "It was a really big deal for him to say it, but I guess you nudged him to tell me then?"

"I did. I felt like if he really wanted a chance with you, as he told me he did, that he needed to be vulnerable to you. Since you were being kind of a jerk and keeping him at arm's length and all. He needed to be breaking down your walls, you understand?"

"Sure and I wasn't being a jerk!" Niamh shot a look of disgust at Gracie. "I was being his friend. Just because a man expresses interest in you doesn't mean you have to reciprocate to protect his feelings, Gracie."

"I don't think she was implying that…" Kira hurriedly interrupted before the conversation could devolve into an argument. "It's likely what she's saying is that you did have feelings for him. So you weren't being true to yourself or him by putting him in the friend zone."

"Well, now, you all make it sound so easy, don't you?" Annoyance rocketed through Niamh and she pulled Rosie closer. "Just tell the famous rugby star who has a bazillion models throwing themselves at him that you fancy him. Sure and he hasn't heard that before right?"

"So you were playing a game then? Playing hard to get?" Gracie asked and Niamh could have throttled her.

"I wasn't playing a game. How could I have known that the man was going to follow me across the country? I haven't even known him all that long, Gracie. I'm still figuring out how I feel about him."

"That's a fair point," Kira interjected again before Gracie could fire something back at Niamh. "This is a new relationship. They're figuring it out. Let them."

"Fine. At least you got your head out of your arse and finally shagged him. I imagine it's been good since you can barely string a sentence together these days what with your head in the clouds and the dreamy look on your face." Gracie finished her wine with a flourish.

"Did I say I liked you? I can't even remember why?" Niamh gaped at Gracie.

"Because we're kin and you have to love me. It's the rule."

"No it is not, as you well know," Niamh said. Rosie shifted in her arms and Niamh let her go so she could walk back to her cushion by the fire. Standing, Niamh brushed off her pants before returning to her seat and grabbing her own glass of wine.

"If you must know...I really like him. He's...he's great," Niamh said simply. She searched for the words of what to say about her feelings for him. "I...he's not just a dumb jock. He's actually really smart. He's interested in my work, and now I can understand even more so why his interest is there. He's well-read, he has a wicked sense of humor, and he is desperately looking for...well, love, I guess. His father is a first-rate jerk, and that's all I'll say about that."

"No mum?" Kira asked, sympathy in her eyes.

"No. It's taking all of my power not to have my mum

adopt him. You know how she is for anything orphaned, what with her own past. It scares me…" Niamh brought a hand to her chest and tried to steady her breathing. "It scares me how quickly he's moved into my life and…if he leaves…it's just. Oh, he'll just leave this giant Mac-sized hole in my heart. I'm actually terrified."

"Why do you think he'll leave you?" Gracie's voice was soft this time.

"Oh, because just look at his life! He's constantly being invited to fancy events. He's in the papers. He travels the world. All this excitement and hype. How would I even fit in? I'm not glamourous or worldly. I want to focus on my books and build a career for myself – one that is meaningful to me. I want to help people. I'm not interested in being a socialite or just some eye-candy on a famous guy's arm."

"Have you guys talked about that? Like what it would be like?"

"There hasn't been a lot of talking." Niamh blushed when the girls high-fived her. "It's still so new and fresh, you know?"

"Ah, I love that stage," Kira sighed. "It's like you're addicted to each other."

"I might still be in it," Gracie mused, her lips pursed in consideration.

"How did he take it when you told him about your own powers?" Kira asked, popping a piece of cheese in her mouth.

"I haven't." Which was another reason Niamh was supremely worried about what their future would be like.

Every time she'd tried to work up the courage to tell him about herself – and the history of the women of the cove – she'd either chickened out or been distracted by Mac's kisses.

"Excuse me?" Gracie said sharply. Rosie jumped up from her bed and padded over to the table. Kira slyly slid the dog a small piece of cheese while Gracie glared at Niamh. "Sure and you're not telling me that the man bared his soul to you and you didn't mention that you're exactly like him?"

"Ah, no. It hasn't come up yet." Niamh smoothed a wrinkle in the tablecloth in front of her.

"Well, now. Here you are worried about your future with him and I can promise you that you won't be having one if you don't come clean to him, Niamh. Men like Mac, they take trust very seriously." Gracie's tone held a sharp warning note.

"There's no reason he shouldn't trust me. I'm not lying to him," Niamh protested – weakly at that.

"You're also not being forthcoming with him. That's not how you build a foundation with someone, Niamh. I'm disappointed in you. What with all that fancy psychology schooling and you can't even see why this is an issue?" Gracie's words wounded her, but not because they called her smarts into question. Because she was right – Niamh needed to be open with Mac.

"Particularly if he's had a hard upbringing, Niamh." Kira reached across the table and squeezed her arm. "He needs to know he has one person in his life that he can count on. That person could be – well, depending how this goes – *should* be you."

"You're right. You're absolutely right. Goddess above, when did I become such a coward?" Niamh muttered.

"You come from a fierce line of warriors, Niamh," Fiona said over her shoulder, causing Niamh to jump and almost knock her wine glass over while Gracie scowled across the table.

"Sure and we've had this talk a time or two, haven't we Fiona? You need to announce yourself in my house."

"I'm here," Fiona said, a saccharine smile on her face.

"A wee bit late, no? She almost knocked wine all over my creams."

"Enough with your mouth. I'm busy right now and can't be bantering with the likes of you." The spirit turned to Niamh. "Niamh. The truth is the only way forward. Love is a gift that, for some, is given but once in a lifetime. It's fragile, and something that can shatter easily. Take care with this man's feelings – you can harm him forever."

"But..I..." Niamh gaped at the empty space in front of her.

"She does love a dramatic exit," Gracie all but growled. "However, she's not wrong."

"I heard that..." Fiona's disembodied voice floated over them.

"Damn her," Gracie hissed and then grinned.

"Okay, okay. You are all correct." Niamh blew out a long breath and gulped the rest of her wine. "The next time I see him – I'll tell him who I am."

"The sooner the better. This can all blow up in your face," Gracie warned.

"I will. I promise. I'm seeing him tomorrow."

"Text me after and tell me how it goes. Well, if you're

not indisposed." Gracie winked lewdly at her and Niamh laughed even though doubt trickled through her.

Would Mac be as accepting of her as she was of him?

CHAPTER 23

*N*iamh started her experiments late that morning, as she'd given herself a chance to catch up on sleep. After she'd come home from Gracie's cottage, it had taken ages to finally drift off to sleep and she'd roundly ignored her alarm that had so rudely tried to awaken her early that morning. Now, it was early afternoon and she was just getting started with her first test of the day.

For this experiment, Niamh wanted to know if she could register the imprint of her energy projecting through the air to move an object. In her head, Niamh envisioned it much like the images seen by a person wearing motion-sensing goggles. Because she was uncertain how psychic energy would read, she wondered if it would give off a heat signature. It wasn't likely, but as with anything, Niamh had to rule possibilities out to add that data to her notes. Getting her equipment ready, Niamh stood back. She made a note of the time and turned on her video camera as well to record any visual elements that could be caught when she slowed the imaging down. Niamh spoke into the camera, quoting the date and the time, and then stepped back and focused on the dinner plate sitting on a table across the room.

If Niamh had wanted to, she could pick the plate up and make it fly across the room at a high rate of speed. But for this experiment, she was going to try her abilities in a slow and steady manner. It was funny, really, to think about how to qualify something that came so naturally to her. Focusing once again, Niamh sent a little mental pulse of energy to the plate and lifted it from the table. Then, she lazily brought the plate, floating through the air, to the middle of the cottage where it hovered about four feet off the ground. Niamh took her time, holding the plate in the air mentally, as she adjusted a few settings on her equipment. Slowly, she rotated the plate.

A flash of movement caught the corner of her eye and Niamh glanced to the small window in the shed door. The window she'd forgotten to pull the curtain over because for the first time in days, meek sunlight filtered through the thin clouds in the sky. Niamh had wanted the light. Now, dread filled her.

Mac's face hovered in the window a look of shock plastered against his features. He turned.

The plate fell to the ground and shattered as Niamh leapt to the door and threw it open.

"Mac! Wait!"

Mac whirled on her; fury having replaced the shock on his features. His mouth worked, as though he was struggling to come up with words, and anxiety twisted low in Niamh's gut.

"Mac. I can explain."

"You…you…" Mac held up a brown bag in his hands. "I was going to bring you a late lunch. Your mum told me you hadn't eaten yet, so I was to come on back. I thought…"

"Mac…" Niamh's voice trembled as Mac blinked at her as though he'd just taken a hard hit on the field.

"You…you were alone in there," Mac said. "Right?"

"Yes, Mac, listen to me…" Niamh approached him, but he took a step back, his hands in the air as though he was protecting himself from her. The movement wrenched Niamh's heart. "I was going to tell you."

"You…you were going to…" Mac shook his head, blinking his eyes rapidly, and then looked back at her. "You were going to tell me? When Niamh? And, what specifically were you going to tell me? That you're like me? That you have powers too? Hmm, I wonder when a good time for that conversation would have been?"

Niamh gasped as Mac chucked the bag of food against the side of the shed, and it exploded open, chips flying everywhere.

"I just…everything happened so fast. We haven't been doing a lot of talking lately."

"We talk all the time Niamh. That's a shite excuse and you know it." Mac paced the garden, vibrating with rage. "I…I shared my very soul with you. A secret that nobody else in the world except my shite father knows. I trusted you. And here you've been what? Making fun of me the whole time?"

"No, Mac. I promise you that wasn't what I was thinking at all. I think you're incredible. You're so very special." Niamh blinked at the tears that rimmed her eyes.

"Oh, sure, I've heard that before. The 'special' kid. You know what that means? The weird one, Niamh!" Mac shouted, his face mottled with red. "The weird kid who has nowhere to go for Christmas. Nobody who shows up at parent meetings at school. Nobody to buy him new clothes. Nobody to teach him how to ride a bicycle or drive a fecking car, Niamh. That's the 'special' kid, Niamh. And you know what? You know what, Niamh?" Mac stopped in front of her, his chest heaving with fury.

"What, Mac?" Niamh's voice was a whisper.

"I thought you'd be different. I thought – *finally* – I've found my person. I've found the one who will accept me through and through. I never thought it could happen for me. Until I met you. I didn't think that I could have that kind of love or acceptance in my life. Until you, Niamh. *You*. You were the one who could see me for me. And now, well, I'm seeing that you never really cared enough to trust me…perhaps I've been a fool all along."

"No, Mac." Niamh was openly crying now. "You're not a fool. This was my fault."

"What then? Am I just someone you could be getting your rocks off with and then be on your way? Have a little fun and move on? You could tell your friends you shagged a famous guy and that's it? Because I shared my world with you, Niamh. And from the beginning you've done nothing but push me away. Finally, I thought, finally – I had broken past your walls. I thought I actually knew you, Niamh. And now I see it was meaningless to you all along."

"That's not true, Mac." Niamh reached out and grabbed his arm but he wrenched it away.

"I don't suggest you be touching me right now." His voice was a dangerous whisper.

"I...I've been scared, Mac. I'm scared of you. Of this. Of us. What this all could mean. I promise you that I was going to tell you today. Even ask Gracie..." As soon as she said the words, Niamh knew she'd screwed up.

"Oh, well, isn't that nice. You and the girls having a wee chat at my expense? Making fun of me then? Even when I expressly asked you to not to speak about what I told you?"

"It wasn't like that Mac, I promise you. Gracie was furious I hadn't told you yet. About me. I realized she was right. That I was being stupid to keep this from you. I'm used to hiding it as well, you know. It's not easy to just tell someone."

"You think I don't know that?" Mac hissed. "Every week I have to do press conferences or magazine interviews. I'm constantly hounded by people asking all sorts of intrusive questions. I've held this secret my entire life. Until you. You were supposed to be different. I thought I could trust you. And yet you're not willing to share that side of yourself with me?"

"I'm so, so sorry, Mac. Please, you have to understand how sorry I am. I know I was weak. I should've immediately told you about myself. I've never... never cared for someone the way that I do you. This has all happened so fast. It scared me. Still scares me." Niamh held a hand to her pounding heart.

"Well, don't worry, Niamh." Mac's eyes were like ice

as he lifted his chin at her. "You've got nothing to be afraid of anymore. We're done here." With that, Mac turned on his heel and, bypassing the house, he disappeared along the garden wall as the skies opened up and rain began to pour down. Niamh stood, frozen, trying to breathe as she watched her heart walk away from her.

Morgan found her there, still standing in the icy rain, tears pouring from her eyes. Drawing her inside, Morgan held Niamh as her pain consumed her.

"We'll fix this, Niamh. I promise you." Morgan rocked her daughter in her arms, soothing her endlessly, as Niamh sobbed on her shoulder.

"I don't think I can," Niamh hiccupped.

"You won't know if you don't try. If you love him, you'll find a way."

"How do I know if I love him?" Niamh asked.

"Because the loss of him will leave a hole in your life that you can never fill."

"I think I feel that way now," Niamh admitted. "I hate that I hurt him."

"Then you have to fix it, Niamh. Take some time to settle down and think about what you really want. Because if you go to him, Niamh? You'd better be damn sure you know what you want. You're either in or you're out. You don't get to play games with his heart."

"I wasn't trying to play games. I didn't think that I was."

"Maybe not. But you were too focused on protecting yourself and your heart to realize that you should have been protecting your relationship with Mac. Because once you love someone, it's not just you anymore, darling.

You've got a responsibility to the relationship. And this time? Well, you've obviously screwed up though I don't know or want the details. But before you try to fix it, you owe it to yourself to get clear on what you want for your future – because judging from Mac's response to you? He's in this – or was – for the long haul. So, you have a choice to make. An important one." With that, Morgan gave her a little shove to the bathroom and Niamh went and crawled into the corner of the shower, bawling her eyes out as the hot stream of water fell on her head, before she finally shuddered to a stop.

Her mother, and Gracie and Kira, were absolutely right. Niamh had never been in a real relationship before and she was used to lads at University playing with her mind. But Mac was no schoolboy, and his feelings for her were very real and almost overpowering. He'd given her his heart to care for, and she'd not understood the gift for what it was.

She needed, no, *had* to fix this.

CHAPTER 24

*M*ac drove furiously up the hill, narrowly avoiding a couple crossing the street. He pulled the car sharply into a parking spot, and all but stormed across the street, catching himself in time before he slammed the door of Gallagher's pub open. Years of being in the public eye kicked in and he did his best to school his emotions.

But apparently, not well enough. Cait took one look at him from across the room as he started to make his way to the courtyard to finish his work for the day and intercepted him.

"Why don't you come have a seat?" Cait asked, wiping her hands with a dish towel.

"I don't want to sit," Mac bit out. He didn't want to be rude to Cait, but he also wasn't feeling particularly civil right now. In fact, a hammer in hand and some good physical work was exactly what he needed to work off this mad.

"Well, we all have to do things we don't want to, don't

we? Since I'm the one paying for you to work on the job, I'll be the one issuing the orders." Cait took his arm and steered him down to the other end of the bar where Mr. Murphy was tucked in his corner. Aside from a few tables finishing up a late lunch, and one man sitting at the other end of the bar, the pub was quiet.

"Hiya, Mac. Good to see you." Mr. Murphy's smile died when he saw Mac's face. "Oh, sure and you look like the wind's been taken out of your sails."

"Hush up for a moment, Mr. Murphy," Cait brought her voice low and where Mr. Murphy would have usually shot back at Cait, he caught the look she threw at them. Mac just stood there, looking between the two, trying to be patient when all he wanted to do was smash every liquor bottle in the place.

"Mac. I need you to listen to me." Cait tapped his arm sharply to bring his gaze down to hers. "Do not look up. But the man at the end of the bar is a reporter."

"Ah, shite," Mac hissed. As though his day couldn't get any worse, he thought. For a moment, he was tempted to go over and confront the man and give him the story he was looking for – Mac Unhinged at Small-Town Pub.

"It's clear you've worked up a head of mad about something. But you can't be blowing off steam in here. Not if you don't want it splashed all over the papers," Cait continued. She began to wipe down the bar like she hadn't a care in the world.

"I…" Mac was still too furious to speak.

"Why don't I show you my community center, boyo? Remember me telling you about it? Now's a grand time to go have a look." Mr. Murphy was already sliding himself slowly from the stool.

"Sure and that's a grand idea. Will you take him, Mac? Careful, he's a bit shaky on his pins."

"That's what I've got my walking stick for, you badger." Mr. Murphy narrowed his eyes at Cait.

"Oh, I just thought that was the stick permanently lodged in your arse," Cait quipped, and Mac shocked himself by laughing. How could he even laugh at a time like this? Cait nodded her approval and motioned for them to go.

"We'll be seeing you later. Thanks for coming to get Mr. Murphy, Mac."

Mac purposely didn't look at the reporter as he helped Mr. Murphy outside, though he was fairly certain they'd be easy to tail as the old man moved at a snail's pace.

"My car is just there. Shall we?" Mac pointed to where his SUV sat at the curb.

"Best to take it if you want to make a getaway. I see the man's trying to settle up his bill, but Cait is chatting him up."

"Good woman."

Once Mac had Mr. Murphy situated, he took off with no particular destination in mind, falling into his habit of going for long drives when he was bothered by something. It wasn't until they'd been driving for a good fifteen minutes did Mr. Murphy finally speak.

"Sure and it's a nice day for a drive, but the center's the other way if you wanted to see it."

"Oh!" Mac punched his fist against the steering wheel. "I'm sorry."

"Nah, don't be. Why don't you take a left up here and follow this road? It'll wind you around the hills a bit before bringing you back into town. I haven't been up this way in a while and I sure do miss the hills."

"You sure?" Mac slanted a glance at him.

"Of course. I've got nothing but time on my hands, lad. And, look, the rain just cleared up. I bet if we get to the top of the hills we'll see a rainbow out over the water."

Like Mac wanted to see rainbows right now. The rain had suited his mood, but there was no reason to take out his anger on the old man. Instead, he took the left as instructed and followed the winding road up through the hills behind the village.

"Woman troubles?" Mr. Murphy broke the silence.

"Why do you say that?"

"I loved my wife, Mac. To her dying breath. I loved her more than life itself." Mr. Murphy's eyes crinkled as he smiled in remembrance. "But there was nobody in this world who could make me madder than she could."

Mac laughed, despite himself, and shrugged.

"Aye, it's a woman thing then."

"I knew it. You had that look about you. Niamh, I'm guessing?"

"That's the one."

"Want to talk about it?" Mr. Murphy asked.

Mac thought about it for a moment. Did he want to talk about it? He never talked when he was mad. He just went to the pitch and worked out until the anger buried itself deep inside him. He'd always been that way. In fact, he positively itched to get out of this car and run laps across the hills until he was so exhausted that he couldn't see straight anymore. It was the only way he knew how to handle his emotions. But now, sitting in his SUV with Mr. Murphy, he began to wonder if there was another way.

"I'm not sure I know how to do that," Mac admitted.

Mr. Murphy seemed to understand what he was trying to say.

"You date a lot, don't you?" Mr. Murphy asked instead.

"Sometimes." Mac shrugged again, keeping his eyes on the slick road ahead of him.

"Anything serious?"

"No." Mac's stomach churned like he'd tried to eat the burnt chicken that he'd attempted to prepare the other week.

"Ah. So probably a lot of fun…but not a lot of arguments?"

"Not really. You shouldn't argue with your partner. What's the point? Dating should be fun," Mac said as they crested the top of a big hill.

Mr. Murphy barked out a laugh and slapped his hand on his leg.

"Of course, dating is fun. Because that's when the person doesn't have any flaws, do they? They can just be the idea you have of them in your head instead of who they really are. But that's not how love actually works."

Mac snorted. Love. He didn't love Niamh. Did he? An icy trickle of fear went through him.

"Well, it's a good thing this isn't love then."

"Isn't it? I have to say…you looked quite into each other on the dance floor a while back. And you've been humming your way into work each day. She's been all smiles when I see her. If it looks like love and talks like love…" Mr. Murphy put his hands in the air.

"I think you're reaching here, Mr. Murphy, I really do."

"There, boyo. Stop the car a moment," Mr. Murphy pointed to where a stone bench sat at the top of the hill. "That's a spot I haven't been to in a while."

"It might come on rain again," Mac said, but he slowed the car and stopped.

"Ah, well. What's a little rain?"

Mac rounded the car and helped Mr. Murphy to the bench where they settled, irrespective of the wet stone.

"See? Didn't I tell you?" Mr. Murphy slapped his arm and pointed to where a double rainbow stretched in a wide arc over the bay. "Isn't she beautiful?"

"Is this where you say something inspirational like there wouldn't be rainbows without the rain and we all need to take the good with the bad?"

"Sure and that's a fine sentiment, isn't it?" Mr. Murphy nodded. "But I think more I'd just say that it's important to appreciate what's right in front of you because in a moment it can all be gone."

As if Mr. Murphy's words had conjured the rain, clouds rolled in further out over the bay, and the rainbow winked from sight.

"She lied to me," Mac bit out.

"I'm sorry for that, I am," Mr. Murphy said after a moment. "It doesn't sound like something Niamh would do, does it?"

"I hadn't thought she would." Resentment crashed

through him. The wall of rain inched closer across the water, but neither man moved.

"Was there a good reason for it?" Mr. Murphy asked. Mac had to appreciate that he wasn't trying to pry the details out of him. Maybe that was why he suddenly felt comfortable enough to open up to the old man.

"Maybe. Maybe not. It's hard to say. I was so mad that I didn't give her much room for explanation. I…I don't care for people easily. Actually, let me say this instead…" Mac held up his hand. "I don't let people close to me easily. All those photos you see? All the women? I barely know their names. I have a few really close friends. I have loads of acquaintances. But I don't let people in."

"Any particular reason?"

"I wasn't taught how to. My whole life…" Mac laughed and shook his head at the advancing wall of rain. "My whole life I was coached how to be on a team. How to run plays. How to be good at the sport of rugby. But nobody taught me how to be in a relationship." His voice cracked. "How to love."

"Well, you're in luck, boyo. You've got the right teacher now." Mr. Murphy surprised him by putting his arm around his shoulders briefly. "And, your first lesson is going to be – there's no right answer when it comes to love."

"What does that even mean?" Mac was oddly moved by the old man's gesture and he leaned into his arm for a moment.

"I just mean that you can't really teach love. Because it's so different for each person. Maybe you love by bringing a girl flowers or writing her a song. Maybe another person loves by sitting by someone's sickbed when they are in need. Love is not a finite resource. It's not something that is only done one way or is used up only on one person or thing. There are a lot of ways to love."

"How do you know when it's the one worth fighting for?" Mac asked. The rain had made its way to the foot of the hills and was encroaching on the village. The wind picked up, bringing with it the salty scent of the ocean.

"I don't think you'd be here asking me that question if it wasn't."

The truth of his words hit home, and Mac did the only thing he could think of to do, he stood and swore roundly. The rain moved faster now, halfway up the hill, and Mac turned to Mr. Murphy.

"We should probably get back in the car."

"Yes, probably." Neither man moved.

"I want to be able to trust her," Mac bit out.

"From my understanding, trust has never been determined when both parties aren't at the same table. Talk to her, Mac."

"I don't want to. It's easier to stay mad."

"Sure, because then you don't have to be vulnerable."

Mac narrowed his eyes at Mr. Murphy's cheerful grin, the first drops of rain hitting the back of his neck.

"I find you kind of annoying," Mac decided.

"Oh well then, you must love me, too," Mr. Murphy said, and Mac threw back his head and laughed as the skies opened above them.

"Come on, old man. Cait will have my head if you catch your death of a chill from this rain." Mac hurried Mr.

Murphy to the SUV and tossed him a towel from the back seat.

"Do you still want to see the center?" Mr. Murphy asked, a shy note in his voice.

"I really would, actually."

By the time they'd finished the tour, Mac's anger had lessened, though the fire of it still burned low in his gut. Mr. Murphy's community center was fast progressing and Mac already had several ideas about how he could help if Mr. Murphy would have him. They made a deal to have a discussion about his formal participation for a day that he wasn't working off a head of mad, and Mac dropped Mr. Murphy back at the pub.

"You sure you don't want to come back in?"

"No, I'm going to go home and get a good workout in. Work off the rest of this anger."

"Don't drink too much. That's never the answer." Mr. Murphy winked at him.

"Hey," Mac said, and Mr. Murphy paused when he was about to close the door. "Thanks for today. I needed it."

"You don't have to figure it all out on your own, Mac. That's what friends are for." Mr. Murphy offered him a kind smile and left, whistling a bouncy tune, as he made his way across the sidewalk and into the pub. Mac pursed his lips and drove up the road, feeling lightness settle over him. Maybe part of his problem came from keeping his own walls up as well. Perhaps he had missed out on many opportunities to love in his life because he'd just kept people back. Musing over that, Mac almost jumped a foot when he heard a voice behind him as he got out of his SUV.

"Hello, Mac."

Mac turned to find Kristie, Fintan's girlfriend, approaching him with a smile and her arms outstretched.

"Kristie…what are you doing here?"

"I just had to see you. Oh, Mac!" Kristie threw herself into his arms and began to cry.

"Come on. Let's get you out of the rain."

CHAPTER 25

*D*on't believe it.

Niamh squinted at the text message on her phone in the early morning light that filtered through a crack in the curtains in her bedroom. It had been a horrible night of sleep for her, and more than once, Niamh had pulled herself from bed and had started to get dressed before stopping herself. She was taking her mother's advice to give Mac just a little space to calm down, before approaching him to talk. Despite the advice, Niamh had still sent him a text message telling him she cared for him and wanted to speak. Niamh wasn't sure that total silence from her would communicate the right message, so at the very least, she didn't want Mac to think she was abandoning him.

Did she get a response? No. Did it make her angry? A little bit. She'd be lying to herself if she said she wasn't. Maybe if she was a better human? But, apparently, she *wasn't* because she'd hurt Mac and now was annoyed that he wouldn't talk to her. Emotions were tricky, and Niamh was humbled to discover that despite her studies, she still had a lot to learn about relationships.

Now, Niamh blinked at Gracie's text message, her brain sluggishly coming awake. What wasn't she supposed to believe?

Believe what?

Her phone rang immediately and Niamh picked it up despite not really wanting to talk to Gracie. If she did, she'd have to admit that she didn't take Gracie's advice and had made a huge mess of things.

"What's up?" Niamh asked, pulling the blanket more firmly around her body. Maybe it was best if she just stayed in bed today and hid from the world. That way her chances of screwing anything else up would be slim.

"I take it you haven't seen the blogs yet."

Dread pooled low in her stomach and Niamh's eyes shot to her phone screen where she registered several notifications on her apps. "I have not. I didn't sleep well. I'm just waking up."

"Do you want me to tell you or do you want to see?"

"I'm going to look either way, so just tell me." Niamh closed her eyes and waited.

"The photos show Mac taking that girl Kristie into his cottage with his arms around her."

"Oh." Niamh felt like she'd been kicked in the gut by the old mule down the way at the farm. "Oh. Well, then. Right."

"Niamh. You can't believe what the press says."

"Right. Right." Niamh kept repeating. "Right then."

"Listen to me. He is not that kind of guy. You have to know that."

"Right," Niamh said, as a wave of nausea washed through her. Gracie didn't know how badly she'd hurt Mac. He had every right to turn to someone else for support.

"Damn it, Niamh. You sound like a parrot. Say something!"

"I think I'm going to be sick," Niamh whispered and hung up the phone before dashing to the bathroom and retching into the toilet. There wasn't much, as she hadn't eaten yesterday after Mac had stormed out, and instead she dry heaved until she could catch her breath. Finally, Niamh stood and splashed cold water on her face and took a swig of mouthwash. Dark smudges ringed her eyes and her skin looked pale and sallow. She should go have a piece of toast and maybe a cup of tea. It would be the adult thing to do. Self-care and all, Niamh lectured herself as she plodded back to bed and pulled the covers over her head. Putting her phone on silent, she ignored Gracie's next few calls as she pulled up the celebrity gossip blogs.

Mac and Kristie – Reunited.

Mac's new lover? The Team Captain's Girl.

Kristie flees back to Mac as Fintan dumps her.

Mac & Kristie – the new power couple?

The bile rose in Niamh's mouth again and she swallowed as she studied the pictures. Sure enough, there was Kristie, looking stunning and as though she had practiced crying in front of the mirror. Nobody looked like that when they cried – if Niamh's face was any testament to that. Single tears streaked down Kristie's cheeks, making her eyes look luminous and beautiful. Whereas Niamh's eyes were bloodshot and swollen after a night of sobbing into her pillow. Kristie clearly wasn't all that broken up over losing Fintan, Niamh sniffed, as she'd hopped right on over to Mac. It didn't matter if she was conniving or merely an opportunist – what mattered was that men fell for it. Particularly, in this case, Mac.

She'd all but given Mac the green light to move on with someone else. Why shouldn't he be with Kristie? For all she knew, Kristie might be just the type of woman Mac needed. At least she went after what she wanted whereas Niamh sulked under her covers with a broken heart. Even Niamh was disgusted with herself.

"Right, then. That's enough of that." Her mother breezed into the room with a tray and put it on the side table next to the bed before pulling the curtains open to let in the wintry grey light. The pouring rain outside perfectly suited Niamh's mood. Niamh pushed herself up so she was sitting against the headboard and looked at the food her mother had brought in. A small bowl of vegetable soup, a few pieces of toast, and a cup of tea crowded the tray and Niamh felt tears well up again. What did she do to deserve such a nice mother?

"No more tears, Niamh. Eat something." Morgan's voice was sharp and Niamh narrowed her eyes at her but followed her instructions and took a bite of toast.

"Thank you," Niamh said after eating in silence for a moment. Her stomach still churned with angst, but at least she didn't feel like she was going to throw up anymore.

"Gracie called me. She's worried about you. Apparently, Mac was photographed with another woman?"

"He was." Niamh ripped a corner off another piece of toast and shoved it in her mouth.

"Well, there's obviously been a mistake."

"Has there? He's kissed her before. You heard him shouting at me yesterday. The man was furious."

"That he was." Morgan sighed and came to sit on the bed next to Niamh, curling up next to her and pulling her into the crook of her arm as though she was a little girl again. "But I'm telling you, Niamh. I just don't see him doing this."

"How can you be sure?" Niamh asked. She leaned into her mother, catching the scent of citrus, and enjoyed the warmth that radiated from her.

"Well, Niamh. You know I have a lot of power. And one of my abilities is to really get a strong read on people. Mac is a man that once he gives his heart…that's it. He'd be too distraught by what happened yesterday to tumble into bed with the next woman. Sure and it's just going against the very essence of who he is as man. You know him, Niamh. Do you really believe that he shagged Kristie?"

Niamh couldn't decide which she was more disgusted at – her mother talking about shagging or the image of Mac with Kristie in bed – and she wrinkled her nose in distaste.

"No," Niamh finally said after a moment of careful consideration. "I think it could be easy to get caught up in all this. It's what the magazines want, anyway, is the drama. I don't think he would do this. But, I could be wrong. I hope I'm not."

"You're not. There has to be another explanation. Why are you even considering this story to be true?"

"I…" Niamh traced her finger along the rose pattern on

the quilt. "I guess because I don't feel like I measure up to someone like Kristie."

"Sure and that's a load of shite."

"Mother!" Niamh laughed softly.

"Well? It is. I get it, Niamh. I know what it's like to feel insecure or like other women are prettier or better than you. But I'm telling you that you need to be putting those insecurities aside. Because my dear darling daughter – you are every bit as good, if not better, than any of those shiny people in the magazines. Maybe they have more money to pay for fancy clothes and glam squads, but I guarantee you, they aren't nicer or happier than you are. This Kristie woman is clearly miserable if she's racing around chasing after any rich lad that will have her. Sounds to me like she has her own personal insecurities – like needing a man to take care of her. You don't have those, Niamh. You know what you want out of life and that's to help people. But now you need to help yourself. You've made a mess of things, and that's on you. Which also means it's on you to clean it up."

"What if…what if I've ruined it all, though? What if he won't take me back?" Niamh turned to look up at her mother. "He'd be in his own right to do so. I broke his trust."

"You didn't break it, but you tarnished it. Lying by omission still hurts and you're going to have to own up to that. It's a harsh learning curve, but I don't think you'll ever make a mistake like this again."

"I just wish I hadn't done it with someone…" Niamh's voice broke as tears threatened again. "With someone I care about."

"I think we can be honest here, right Niamh? It's just us…" Morgan squeezed her more tightly. "Sure and I could be reading this wrong, but it's more than just caring for him."

"I know. I just can't say it out loud, Mum. The first time I do needs to be for him."

"Then that's what you'll do then. Come now, let's have ourselves a nice little afternoon and we'll get you ready to go see him."

"But…what if Kristie is there?"

"Kick her arse right on out, Niamh. Come on now. You've had twenty-four hours to mope. You know that's my time limit." Her mother had always allowed Niamh to wallow in her feelings for one whole day whenever something had upset her, but after that time point Morgan had always nudged Niamh toward taking steps forward out of the well of sadness.

"You're right. Honestly, even *I'm* getting annoyed with myself. I certainly screwed up and I'm woman enough to own that. Hell, I'll even grovel. But as Fiona has not-so-delicately reminded me, we've warrior blood running through our veins. It's time for me to go get my man."

"That's my girl!" Morgan glanced at the slim gold watch on her wrist. "Well, not this second. He's likely working at the pub and unless you want the entire village eavesdropping on your conversation, I suggest you wait a few more hours."

"What am I supposed to do until then?"

"We'll pick a stunning outfit for you to wear to make Mac drool. Otherwise, might I suggest you spend a little time in your shed writing your thoughts down? Or at the very least getting clear on what you want to say to him? This might be your only shot, and I don't want you to blow it."

"I'm beginning to think you're planning to adopt Mac whether I'm with him or not…" Niamh grumbled.

"Well, now, that's a lad crying out for some mothering if I've ever seen one. I don't suspect I'll stop inviting him to dinner anytime soon. We're friends outside of you, you know." Morgan got off the bed and crossed the room to open Niamh's closet.

"So it's like that, then, eh? Stabbed in my back by me own mother," Niamh pulled a deep Irish accent and put the back of her palm to her forehead like a damsel in distress.

"It's a ruthless world we live in, Niamh. Best get used to it."

CHAPTER 26

*N*iamh's gut twisted in knots as she pulled her mum's car to a stop at Mac's rental cottage. For a moment, she just sat there, willing him to come racing outside with a smile on his face, so that she could avoid the whole groveling part that she wasn't looking forward to. Personal growth, Niamh reminded herself. The hardest part about making mistakes was owning up to them. Niamh flipped the sun visor down and checked her makeup once more and smiled, making sure she hadn't mysteriously gotten something in her teeth in the ten minutes since she'd brushed them.

Initially, Niamh had pulled out slick leather leggings that hugged every inch of her curves and a lace top, but Morgan had vetoed the look stating that Niamh shouldn't look like she was on the prowl – but instead needed to be warm and welcoming. Together they'd decided on a vintage wrap dress with a soft floral print in muted shades of gold, pink, and deep red. Niamh had wrapped a wide brown leather belt around her waist and matched it with chunky knee-high boots. They'd styled her hair so that it tumbled casually around her shoulders and down her back, and Niamh had hung large gold hoops in her ears. Morgan had pressed a rose quartz necklace on her, citing its properties for encouraging love, and Niamh had paid careful attention to her makeup. All in all, while she couldn't afford the newest and fanciest designers, Niamh felt beautiful because this outfit reflected exactly who she was. She didn't go in for trends or brand names but took her time with selecting her clothes carefully.

Much like her men, Niamh supposed, as her mind danced back to all the boys she'd dated before. And, they had been boys – hadn't they? Compared to Mac's virility and willingness to be open and vulnerable with her, the guys she'd dated in University paled in comparison. This man was real, he was hers, and she knew in her heart of hearts that she would want no other. Taking a deep breath, Niamh straightened her shoulders and got out of the car. The night was cool, but thankfully dry, and a few stars had begun to sparkle in the velvety softness of twilight.

Niamh marched to the door before she could chicken out and knocked loudly. Waiting, she looked around, smiling when she saw that Mac had hung his team's flag in one of the windows. Knocking again, Niamh waited. When several minutes passed, her heart fell. She hadn't planned for what to do if the man wasn't home. Should she just wait on his doorstep? Niamh blinked down at her phone and then pulled up his number to call him.

The call rang through to voice mail and Niamh hesitated for a second before speaking.

"Hi, Mac. It's me. Niamh, ah, that is. I'm here. At

your doorstep. I needed to see you. I need to talk to you. I know you don't want to see me and I know I hurt you and I'm the worst person in the world. But…I just…I have something to tell you. In person, that is. Not to your voicemail. And I'd very much like the chance to do that. But if you don't want to give me that chance, I guess I'll have to respect that as well. I just…I miss you…" Niamh hung up before she could ramble anymore and then cursed. Perhaps not the most eloquent of voicemail messages. Sighing, she did the only thing that a person did when they were nursing a heartbreak in Grace's Cove – Niamh went to Gallagher's Pub.

Why was this damn pub always so busy? Niamh thought as she nodded to a few people she knew and beelined to the corner of the bar where only a few stools were left.

"There's a lovely lass on a cold winter's evening. Come on down and brighten an old man's day." Mr. Murphy patted the stool next to him and Niamh joined him reluctantly. She wasn't particularly in the mood to talk, but sometimes with Mr. Murphy, all a body had to do was nod and listen as he reminisced on one story or another. Niamh hoped it was one such night.

"Whiskey. Green Spot. Neat." Niamh said to the bartender who stopped down at her corner. Cait was nowhere to be seen, but Niamh supposed the woman deserved a night off once in a while. "Would you like one?"

"Sure and I'm enjoying my pint. Thank you though."

Niamh just nodded and lapsed into silence. When her

drink came she held a finger up to the bartender and took it down in one fiery gulp.

"Keep them coming. Please," Niamh amended when she realized she sounded a bit demanding.

"Tough day?" Mr. Murphy asked. He looked particularly dapper tonight in a grey tweed vest over a heather wool sweater.

"You look nice tonight, Mr. Murphy. Have a hot date?" Niamh changed the subject. She nodded her thanks when the bartender returned with the bottle and just stood there while Niamh took down another glass and then refilled it before walking away.

"I'm sitting next to you, aren't I?" Mr. Murphy winked at her and Niamh smiled.

"Well, then, seeing as how I'm unattached, it looks like you've won yourself a date tonight."

"Sure and I'm a lucky man, I am at that." A light lilting string of notes went up from across the room and Niamh glanced back to see a trio of musicians had tucked themselves in the front booth. Lovely, she thought. Couldn't a woman brood in silence these days? Despite the way the whiskey churned – a hot ball of fire in her stomach – Niamh finished her next and signaled the bartender. She could ignore the stomach pain in order to relish the numbness that alcohol was beginning to provide.

"You must be Niamh."

Niamh glanced to the woman who slid onto the stool next to her, and grimaced.

"For feck's sake," Niamh muttered into her glass.

"Yes, well, I'm not particularly happy to be stuck another night in this boring little town either," Kristie said, smiling up at the bartender. "Vodka soda with slice of lime please."

"Surely there's someplace else for you to sit?" Niamh asked. Kristie's hair was glossy in the light from overhead, and her manicure was perfect. Niamh glanced down at her own chipped nails and curled her fingers into her palms.

"There are no boring places – only boring people," Mr. Murphy said with an easy smile. Niamh waited for Kristie to be rude to him so she could eviscerate her, but the woman looked suitably chastened instead.

"What do you want?" Niamh asked, not feeling the need to be polite. It could be the whiskey. Or it could be that this woman had just thrown herself at Mac. Likely a combination of the two, really.

"Listen, Niamh…" Kristie squeezed her lime into her drink and then delicately wiped her fingers with a bar napkin. "I don't know you."

"And I'd prefer to keep it that way." Her mother would be appalled at her manners right now, but Niamh found she just didn't care.

"I don't think we run in the same circles, darling." Kristie looked her up and down and Niamh just rolled her eyes.

"In academia, you mean? No, we certainly don't." Niamh took another sip of her whiskey while Kristie scrunched up her nose to think about Niamh's words.

"Whatever. The point is…you've won."

"I didn't realize we were playing a game." Niamh fully turned to Kristie now, rocking a little on her stool as a wave of dizziness rushed over her. She definitely should have eaten more than just the toast.

"Oh please, don't act like you weren't trying to grab the headlines away from me," Kristie laughed outright, shaking her shiny mane of hair as she did. "Even I know a master operator when I see one. Sure and you played it cool, didn't you? Getting Mac to follow you here was certainly a power move on your part."

"I…" Niamh's mouth gaped open as fury worked its way through her. "I did no such thing." Turning, she motioned to the bartender only to see Cait's mutinous face on the other side of the bar with a glass of water in hand.

"Have a glass," Cait ordered.

"I'll have a whiskey, Cait."

"Aye, you will. After you have this water."

"Looks like you'd better do as she says or you'll get sent to bed early." Kristie snickered and then stilled when Cait leaned across the bar and stopped inches from her face.

"Mind your manners in my pub, or I'll be seeing you out the door."

"Yes, ma'am." Kristie instantly dropped her head.

Niamh was inclined to make a snarky comment back, but the steel in Cait's gaze had her instead taking a sip of her water. Cait gave them both a withering look before stomping off to the other end of the bar.

"Well, she's right terrifying, isn't she?"

"She is at that. Good to have on your side in a bar fight, though."

Kristie snorted and despite herself, Niamh smiled.

"Listen, Niamh. I don't want to like you, but since I'm here and need a drinking buddy, you'll have to do."

"Gee, thanks. Is there anyone else who can sign up for

that position? I'm sure there's a few lads around here that would be happy to fill my stool."

"I'm taking a break from men. I only came down here to make Fintan jealous."

"Why?" Niamh looked at Kristie in exasperation, finally seeing what her mother had been saying all along about the woman. A deep insecurity flashed behind her tawny eyes. "Why not just stay and be a good partner to him? It was clear the man was besotted with you."

"You think so?" Kristie twirled a lock of hair around her finger. "I just felt like he never gave me much attention."

"I mean…he's a busy man. Right? Like all the team demands and stuff. Isn't that part of what goes with it?"

"I suppose," Kristie pushed out her lower lip in a pout. "I just want to spend more time with him. I get bored easily."

"As Mr. Murphy so delicately pointed out – isn't that your problem? Not Fintan's?" Niamh asked and watched as Kristie appeared to have an epiphany on the spot. A lightness came over her face.

"You're saying that if I find something to do with my time, I won't rely on Fintan so much?"

"Yes, I am." Niamh shook her head. "It's your responsibility to follow something that you are passionate about in life."

"Well, I'm passionate about…" Kristie began and Niamh cut her off.

"Not Fintan. We all know you're passionate about men. I'm talking about something else that is yours alone. School. Classes. A hobby. Fashion…" Niamh studied

Kristie's outfit again. "You could learn to be a stylist or something like that if you enjoy it."

"I can get paid to dress people?" Kristie's eyes lit up as she turned and looked at Niamh again.

"Not me. Other people. Go find rich people who dress poorly. Make them look good. You'll certainly find a clientele through word-of-mouth if you do a good job and stop doing stupid shite like lying to men and playing with their emotions."

"Huh, I never thought about that." Kristie pursed her lips and tapped a finger against them. Niamh wasn't sure if she was referring to being a stylist or stopping her lies, but she didn't care. When Cait ducked into the kitchen she flagged the other bartender for a quick top-off.

"What did I win, by the way?" Niamh asked, taking down the whiskey before Cait came back out and lectured her. The night began to take on a fuzzy quality where voices grew louder and the music made her start to tap her boot on the stool footrest.

"Mac, of course. He never wanted me, you know."

Niamh just shrugged a shoulder, uncertain of how to respond.

"That night at the club? I tipped the press off and waited outside. I threw myself at him and kissed him. He was furious, you know. Went right back inside and told Fintan. Boy, did I get in trouble for that one." Kristie shook her head. "It was bold even for me."

"What…then why are you back down here?" Niamh's mind whirled as she realized she'd just sort of accepted the kiss between them to be fact. It was something she had expected of Mac the Playboy as she'd first thought of him before she'd gotten to know him better.

"Fintan and I had another big fight. I just thought I'd stir things up a bit."

"How's that working out for you?"

"Not great," Kristie admitted, "but maybe this trip wasn't a waste after all. You've given me some things to think about. Maybe I'll just take some time off men all together and see where it takes me. Focus on myself for once."

"Sure and that's probably a good thing," Niamh said softly, wondering if she needed to do the same.

"Anyways, I'll say this – the man has it bad for you. If I was really into Mac? Well, I'd be devastated. Be a good lass now and put that on your tab, will ya?" Kristie stood and patted Niamh's shoulder before strutting from the pub. A part of Niamh – the tipsy part – wondered if she'd just hallucinated the entire encounter.

"Was she just…" Niamh took a sip of her whiskey and turned to Mr. Murphy. Except he was no longer there. Mac was.

She spit out her whiskey.

CHAPTER 27

"*S*ure and that's not a nice way to greet someone." Mac grabbed a napkin and brushed at his pants.

He looked wonderful, Niamh thought, drinking him in. His hair was damp, as though he'd just showered, and the light blue Henley he wore made his eyes look bright in his handsome face. Niamh wanted to crawl into his lap and never let go. Instead, she looked away, heat creeping up her face.

"I'll be apologizing for that." Among other things, Niamh thought silently. Just add it to her list of transgressions.

"But nothing else?" Mac asked and Niamh whirled on him, the anger she'd kept neatly at bay with Kristie firing through her body.

"Well I was trying to apologize, wasn't I? But somebody wasn't home. And somebody doesn't answer text messages. And somebody doesn't answer phone calls. Or respond to voicemails. And instead leaves me crying in the rain." Niamh's voice was rising, but she found she didn't care.

"Now, then, I'm entitled to take some time to think about things," Mac said, keeping his own voice low as he glanced around at the interested faces in the pub.

"In the arms of Kristie?" Niamh shot back and then winced. She held up a hand before he could speak. "I know it's not what it looks like. I get it. But honestly, Mac? It's just fecking annoying. If it's not her, then it will be some other girl, won't it? They follow you everywhere like you're the fecking pied piper of models. How the hell am I supposed to be competing with that?" Niamh was definitely not using her inside voice and the music came to a halt as everyone stopped pretending not to eavesdrop and settled in for some entertainment.

"Sure and you can't be blaming me for the actions of others now, can you, darling?" Mac asked, crossing his arms over his chest as he rocked back on his stool.

"Don't you *darling* me. I'm sick of everyone patting me on the head like I'm some precious little puppy. I. Am. A. Woman!" Niamh punctuated the words by poking Mac in the chest and then almost fell off her stool. Mac caught her in time and eased her back so that she was steady once more. Which, for some reason, annoyed her even more. Like she needed him to take care of her?

"I'm certain myself and every other red-blooded male in here can be attesting to the fact that we see you're a woman. Isn't that right lads?" Mac asked around, no longer bothering to pretend he didn't know that everyone was listening. A chorus of voices agreed with him.

"Well, I'm sick of it. I don't want women throwing

themselves at you. I don't want newspapers following us. Yeah, I'm looking at you, buddy," Niamh called loudly down to where the reporter sat at the end of the bar, notepad in front of him. "You must have a very lonely life."

"Okay, let's not insult the reporters," Mac cringed, raising a hand in apology to the man at the end of the bar. "They're just doing their job."

"It's a crummy one," Niamh insisted, loudly.

"Niamh. Let's get you out of here. We can talk," Mac said, clearly realizing that this conversation was not going to end well.

"Oh, now he wants to talk?" Niamh addressed the crowd. "This man left me crying in the pouring rain. He wouldn't even let me apologize. Can you believe that?"

"Aww, come on, Mac. Let the lass apologize," a man from the crowd called out.

"I plan to. In fact, I'm happy to make her grovel. But not here and not when she's…how many whiskies in?" Mac glanced to the bar.

"Six or so?" The bartender called and then hunched his shoulders at Cait's exclamation.

"You poured more for her?" Cait asked. "She can't handle her liquor."

"What I can't handle…" Niamh stood and grabbed the side of the bar when her knee buckled. That was odd. "What I can't handle is when I can't fix things. And this man doesn't want to fix things. He doesn't care about me. I'm just another woman in his rotation. With cheaper shoes." Niamh looked sadly down at her boots and almost toppled forward when she did.

"That's it." Mac stood up and Niamh's world went upside down when he grabbed her and threw her over his shoulder.

"Mac!" Niamh squealed, a wave of dizziness almost making her pass out.

"You show her Mac!"

"Let her apologize!"

"I bet she'll…" That one got cut off at Cait's sharply worded reprimand, and then Niamh felt the cool night air hit her face as the door closed on a chorus of cheers.

"I can't…" Niamh tapped his leg weakly. "Too dizzy."

Immediately, Mac switched her position so that he carried her in his arms like a man carrying his bride over the threshold. Niamh blinked at a group of people who openly gaped at them, and took a few deep breaths to steady herself until the dizziness passed. Mac, for his part, said nothing as he pounded up the hill, barely breathing heavily as he made his way to his rental cottage. Niamh was once again reminded just how strong he was as he held her like she was as light as a rugby ball.

Mac didn't put Niamh down when he got to his door, instead he switched her to one arm while he got his key out, and then nudging the door open with his leg, he walked inside and dropped her on the couch before crossing the room to flip on some lights. Niamh bounced on the leather and was immediately reminded of the first time they'd made love. Here. At the memory of what they'd had, tears flooded her eyes.

"Wait, wait, wait. Hold on." Mac jumped to attention. He ran into the kitchen and got a roll of paper towels, a glass of water, and a pizza box. Returning to the couch, he sat down next to her and offered her all three at once.

"Pizza?" Niamh hiccupped, as the tears fell faster.

"Might soak up some of the alcohol?" When Niamh didn't take a slice, he closed the box and put it on the floor before handing her a paper towel. She took it and held it to her eyes but couldn't seem to stop the flood of tears. Stupid alcohol. Stupid relationships. Stupid love.

"Why do you think love is stupid?"

"Am I talking out loud?" Niamh gasped.

"You were, yes."

"I'm just...oh Mac. I'm a mess. I really screwed up and I'm terrified to lose you, but I'm also scared of what being with you will be like and I don't know what to do." Niamh held her hand to her chest, where her heart felt like it was beating a thousand beats per minute. "I feel so much here and it hurts. I hate that I hurt you. You have to know how sorry I am. I'm so so sorry."

"I know you are, Niamh. You need to calm down. Here, focus on your breathing."

Niamh's chest had begun to heave as the possibility that she had well and truly lost him raced through her, and panic scrambled at her core. When his arms came around her, pulling her close, she buried her face in his chest.

Niamh blinked at the sunlight, her thoughts slow and sticky like honey, her throat dry. She swallowed and pressed herself up, trying to figure out where she was.

In Mac's bed.

The events of the night before came crashing over her, and Niamh fell back to the bed, burying her face in the pillow for a moment. Thankfully, the bed was empty, giving Niamh a moment to collect herself. She cringed as the scene of the pub came back to her – not to mention the reporter sitting at the end of the bar – Niamh could only imagine what was printed in the blogs today. The rest of the night was fuzzy, and the last thing she remembered was crying on Mac's couch. Oh no…what had she said?

Sitting up, Niamh listened for a moment before slipping from the bed and padding quickly to the bathroom. The sight in the mirror that greeted her was…well, it wasn't her finest moment. Niamh glanced down at the simple grey sports t-shirt that Mac must have changed her into and glowered at the dark circles of mascara that ringed her eyes. The man had undressed her and put her to bed and she'd yelled at him in a pub and then cried on him.

Well, they'd had a nice go while they'd lasted, Niamh decided as she took a swig of mouthwash. Now she just needed to slip out the back door and move to a new country so she could hide from this particular embarrassment. Gingerly, Niamh opened the door and almost shrieked to find Mac standing there with a dish towel on his shoulder and a glass of water in his hand.

"Sure and you're trying to take me to an early grave then," Niamh gasped, hand at her heart.

"Here's some water. And some tablets for your headache." Mac held up two pills before surprising Niamh by leaning over and kissing her forehead gently. "I'm just finishing breakfast. Meet me in the kitchen. I'm keeping your clothes hostage, so you can't go anywhere."

Niamh gaped at Mac's broad back as he wandered away in a loose t-shirt and plaid sleep pants. Could the man read minds as well? Swallowing the pills with the water, Niamh walked slowly to the kitchen and reminded herself that running from her problems never solved anything. And right now? Aside from her massive headache, that is, figuring out what happened last night with Mac was her biggest one. Oh, and apologizing, that is. She still wasn't entirely certain if she'd managed to formally apologize to Mac yet.

Stupid alcohol. Niamh had never been able to hold her liquor, which is why she generally stuck to wine and never too much of it. This was why, Niamh reminded herself. Because she ended up with no pants on in the kitchen of a man who held her heart in his hands.

"I was beginning to think you'd sleep all day," Mac said when Niamh came to the doorway. "Juice? Coffee? Tea?"

"Coffee, please." The caffeine might make the pills work faster. Why was he being so nice to her? She was the one who had screwed up.

"Go on then, I'll bring it to the couch." Niamh remembered how he hated his kitchen chairs.

"Mac...did we?"

"Have sex? No, Niamh. We just slept next to each other."

"Oh...but, I mean what did I...did we talk?"

"Go sit down. We'll talk in a second. I could eat four pizzas the way I feel right now." Mac began stacking toast on a tray and Niamh took him at his word. Going to the couch, she pulled the fuzzy blanket from the back and curled it around her legs. A moment later, Mac appeared with a tray that was towering with food and put it on the cushion between them. Niamh took her cup of coffee and a piece of toast, watching as Mac bit into a sausage roll.

"You cook now?" Niamh asked.

"Nah, picked these up this morning and just heated them up when I heard you moving around."

"Oh, you were up and out already?"

"Yup. Got a workout in, too," Mac said cheerfully.

How was he so cheerful when she felt like her world was unraveling at the seams? Niamh dutifully ate her piece of toast, and then leaning back on the cushions, she studied him. This did not look like a broken-hearted man to her. So either he didn't actually care for her or Mac had come to some conclusion about their future – unbeknownst to her. Either way, it was too much for her to bear.

"Mac, I don't remember what happened last night after I came home and cried on your couch. It's clear that something did or you wouldn't be this cheerful. I don't drink like that often, so I apologize for...anything that I might have said or did. Did we talk?"

"No, we didn't, Niamh. You passed out in my arms and I put you to bed. You're not kidding about being a lightweight. You went from crying and talking to snoring in about three seconds flat." Mac grinned at her while heat flooded Niamh's cheeks.

"Lovely. Well, then, let's just get this over with." Niamh had been practicing what she was going to say to Mac ever since he had stormed away from her and she needed to get it out. And then hopefully go find a quiet corner where she could collect her dignity.

"That doesn't sound inviting."

"Mac..." Niamh forced herself to look at where he'd

paused with a sausage roll in hand. "I really screwed up. Badly. I wish that I had a better explanation for it or that I could validate my reasonings, but I really don't. There was no excuse for me not sharing my gifts with you when you chose to be open with me. I can't even rightly say why I didn't. Habit, maybe? But I suspect that's just an excuse. If I really wanted to dig deep, and if you really needed an explanation, then I would say it's likely because the idea of us…of you…scares me so much that I was self-sabotaging. I didn't believe in us, so I subconsciously found a way to blow it up before you could hurt me."

"Niamh…" Mac said. He put the sausage roll down and moved the tray of food to the floor. He didn't touch her, which she appreciated, but instead just looked at her patiently. "Tell me why you're scared of me. Of us."

"I'm scared that one day you'll wake up and look at me and realize that I don't fit. That I'm not really a part of your world. You need someone like Kristie, Mac." Niamh hurried on when a flash of annoyance ripped across Mac's face. "Maybe not her, but someone like her. Someone who is going to look fancy for your events? Who will look good on your arm. Who will network with all the right people and say all the right things at all the galas and clubs and whatever else it is you do. It's not my world, Mac. And I fear that…for a while you're going to think this is fun, but then one day you'll realize that I can't be what you need me to be and then you'll…"

"I'll what?"

"You'll leave me." Niamh's voice caught. "And that's the part that I don't think I can bear at all."

"So basically you're worried you might drown so

you're never going to dive in the water. Is that what I'm getting?"

"Something like that."

"Do I even get a say in this?" For the first time that morning, the cheerful note left Mac's voice. "Or is it just you over there making the decisions for us? You have decided that you know what I need and since you think you're not it – then that's it then? You're out the door and I'm left with what?"

"You'll find someone else," Niamh shrugged and jumped when Mac threw a cushion across the room. Instinctively, Niamh caught the cushion with her mind and stopped it before it shattered a pretty vase that was tucked on a side table by the door. They both stared at where the pillow hovered in mid-air before Niamh let it fall gently to the floor.

"Why do you think you're so replaceable, Niamh? When you're clearly a goddess?" Mac's voice rasped with emotion and Niamh felt her heart begin to crack.

"Mac…"

"No, you had your say. Now I get mine." Mac stood and began to pace, clearly too agitated to sit still. "Everything you said about what I need is wrong. You're still thinking that I am the Mac you see in the papers, but not the person standing before you, Niamh. Sure, there's fancy events and the press hounds me – that's just part of it. But all the stuff you mentioned? It was about looks. How would someone look on my arm in the press? It wasn't about what I needed or wanted in my life. I don't care – I'm happy to go to the galas alone and come home to you if that's not your thing. And for what it's worth – I think you're the most stunning woman I've ever seen in my life. I would be proud to have you on my arm wherever we go. But what I really need? I need someone who supports me. Who makes me laugh. Who astounds me with her smart mind and interesting studies. Who has a depth of empathy and caring unlike any women I've met. A woman I can trust with my secrets, with my happiness, and with my future. I need someone who isn't going to think I'm strange or terrifying when I catch a vase from falling or swerve long before a dog runs out in the street. I need someone who thinks I'm special because of who I am, not despite it."

Niamh blinked up at Mac as he came to kneel before her, grimacing for a moment, and then meeting her eyes again. His hands were warm on her legs as he leaned closer.

"I need a woman that I can trust with my heart. You're it, Niamh."

"You really don't care if I skip out on VIP nights at the club?" Niamh asked, her voice watery.

"Never have to go to one again. Hell, the only reason I go is so I don't have to be alone. But with you – I'm never alone."

"I…I love you, Mac. It astounds me the depth of feeling I have for you. It's terrifying and all-encompassing and I don't even know how I'd take my next breath if I knew you weren't in my life."

"I know you do, Niamh. I had a very wise person help bring me around to understanding what happened between us. I'm sorry I didn't respond to your text messages. I needed some time to collect my thoughts. I won't do that to you again, I promise. Niamh, I love you. I really, really love you. I know my fame can be overwhelming, but at the end of the day – I'm just me. Say you'll take a chance on me?"

"Of course, I will Mac. I really do love you." A trickle of excitement went through Niamh and she giggled, feeling like a weight lifted off her shoulders. "I love you! Oh, it's fun to say."

"With you I've found what I'm looking for, Niamh. I won't be alone anymore." Mac kissed her, pouring his love into it, and Niamh melted into him until he made an odd noise.

"What's wrong?"

"I, um…I knelt in the sausage rolls."

Niamh threw her head back and laughed as Mac picked her up and carried her to the bedroom.

EPILOGUE

"*I* still can't believe you bet on me." Niamh shot Gracie a look heavy with annoyance. "It doesn't feel fair. You had insider information."

"You're just mad because I got some pretty new boots out of it." Gracie looked down at her chunky-soled sparkly Doc Martens and smiled. "I love these boots."

"They suit you, that's for sure."

It was hard for her to be annoyed at Gracie because Niamh was just so happy. After the initial flurry of interest in her and Mac's relationship, the press had largely left them alone once there weren't any scandalous stories to follow. Now, the blogs were all focused on who Fintan was dating – and with a new woman on his arm every week, the team captain was keeping the reporters busy. Niamh was grateful to subside into relative oblivion, as she and Mac enjoyed nights cooking at home or going for long drives on rainy Sunday afternoons.

In the months since they had been together, Niamh had finished her studies and submitted her final work to her panel. Now, she was waiting to defend her thesis and it was only a matter of time, hopefully, before she could advance her career. Niamh was already scoping out spots for a small office and was torn between working in Dublin or out of Grace's Cove. Mac, after spending more time in the village, had fallen in love with it and was currently looking at houses to buy there. It still made Niamh a little giddy, to think about how far their relationship had progressed, when this time last year she had been a lonely university student.

"I can't believe you managed to drag me to a match," Gracie sniffed and looked around at the crowded stadium. They sat in an area sectioned off for players' families and Niamh had slowly gotten to know a few of the other spouses. It was beginning to feel like a little family, and Niamh had finally taken the time to learn the sport of rugby so she wouldn't make a fool of herself at games.

"There he is. The love of my life." Gracie beamed up at Dylan who had returned with a box of popcorn.

"I'm so grateful you're dating Mac," Dylan grinned down at Niamh as he passed the popcorn to Gracie. "It's making it a lot easier to drag Gracie from the cottage and to a proper city once in a while."

"Sure and it's annoying, isn't it? But, I have to admit, Dublin's growing on me a bit. For short visits, of course."

"I think you're both managing to live the best of both worlds," Niamh said with a smile.

"As are you and Mac. Oh look! There he goes!" Gracie jumped up and screamed, scattering popcorn everywhere.

"Sure and she hates these matches, too, doesn't she?" Niamh said to Dylan who laughed.

Niamh's heart caught as Mac ran out onto the field, his eyes darting up to the stands where she sat, his smile all for her. He still continued to take her breath away – even when he just walked in the apartment after coming home from training. Now, watching him take the field, pride filled her.

"I've been meaning to tell you, Niamh. Gracie and I have done some digging, along with some past-life visits, and we've discovered my daughter from that time period." Dylan lowered his voice and leaned into Niamh as he spoke. "Sure and it hurts me to know that she never knew of me."

"And…Mac is part of that family?"

"It seems so. I think we might be able to track them to today. I need to do some more digging, of course, as well as see if Mac would be open to discovering more family."

"I…I think he might be. It's a vulnerable point for him in his life, so I'll need to talk to him and see if he's open to it. Plus, we have to keep in mind what that would look like in the papers, of course. Maybe even just knowing that he isn't so alone might be enough for him. I can't speak for him…" Niamh shrugged.

"Well, it appears Grace's love was so strong for me, and her family, that her magickal enchantment extended far past what we'd ever thought. Which is doing this one's head in…I'll tell you that." Dylan smiled up at Gracie who was still standing and looking nervously toward the field. "I believe she's come to view herself as the grounding point for all of you with extra abilities. Now, discovering that we might have missed a whole family branch, well, it's going to be hard to stop her from reaching out. If Mac says not to, I'm sure she'll figure out a way to make contact without revealing the connection to Mac, of course."

"Actually, I might want in on that," Niamh said, her tone serious. "If there are kids out there with abilities that they are struggling to understand, well, that's right in my wheelhouse. Keep me in the loop on this, will you?"

"Of course. Let me know when you speak to Mac about it as well."

"Sure and that's no problem. I'll bring it up to him somewhere when his world isn't dominated by rugby. Which likely won't be anytime soon." Niamh jumped to her feet and screamed when they scored a try.

After the game, which they won, Niamh made plans to meet up with Gracie and Dylan for dinner after she went down to the locker room to wait for Mac in the hallway. When he came out, dressed in a team track suit and his hair still wet from the showers, Niamh's heart swelled at the sight of him.

"There's my girl." Mac grabbed her and, lifting her up, he swung her in a circle before holding her tight so her body slid down his muscular front. Heat immediately flared and Niamh blushed as her mind went blank for a moment.

"Great match," Niamh finally said. She leaned into his kiss, not caring if the reporters were watching, and was a little dizzy when they finally broke apart.

"We've work to do. We almost didn't squeeze that one out. But I'm pleased." Mac took her hand and they strolled from the building to the private lot for the players to park in.

"Mac! Going to the club tonight? We'll be there!" Fintan called out from where he'd stopped in front of a sleek black Mercedes. The men had patched things up fairly quickly after Mac had come back to Dublin, and the team was the better for it when Kristie had decided to stop sniffing around the players. The last Niamh had heard was that she was making a go of it as a stylist and Niamh actually genuinely wished success for her. Well, kind of. She still didn't care for the woman. But Niamh was working on being a better person these days.

"Nah, I've got dinner plans." Mac waved away the invite easily enough and Niamh's heart fluttered in her chest as Mac stopped and opened the passenger door for her.

"It doesn't bother you, does it? Missing out on the time with your mates?" Niamh stopped and looked up at him.

"Niamh. I see these guys all day every day. I don't need to see them every night, too."

"Oh, sure. I just…I don't want people to think I've forced you to settle down or anything." Periodically, insecurity still reared its ugly head for Niamh, but she was working on it.

"Do you honestly think anyone believes that I could be forced to do anything?" Mac asked, towering over her all muscles and stubbornness.

"I mean…most people couldn't. But I know that I can…" Niamh stood on her tiptoes and whispered a particularly naughty suggestion in his ear.

"Yep, that'll do it. Your wish is my command, my goddess."

Their life wasn't perfect, and Niamh didn't need it to

be, but in this moment? She couldn't think of anything that would make her happier.

"I'm so glad that you're my friend." Niamh still teased Mac about being in her friend-zone for a while.

"You're really the best buddy I've ever had."

"Mates for life." Niamh laughed the whole way to the restaurant.

What do you think is up next for Mac & Niamh? Will the cove glow blue for their love?

Join my newsletter and I will send you a free Mac and Niamh short story.

"One Year Later"
... discover if he's ready to pop the big question or not!

www.triciaomalley.com/story

Save the Fae Princess or save his powers? Fae warrior,
Nolan, must choose between loyalty and love in this
addictive new Irish romance series. Reunite with fan-
favorite characters from the Isle of Destiny & Mystic Cove
books.

A brand new series from Tricia O'Malley!

**Read on for a sneak-peak of Chapter One from Song of
the Fae**
Book 1 in the Wildsong Series

CHAPTER 1

*T*he door to Gallagher's Pub slammed open with such force that the musicians tucked in the front booth fell silent and the crowd gaped as a man strode in from the storm that raged outside.

The Prince of Fae had arrived.

Judging from the furious wave of energy that crackled around him, as though he controlled the very storm itself, Prince Callum was ready for battle.

"Oh shite," Bianca breathed from where she sat, tucked in a booth next to her husband Seamus, along with Callum's right-hand man, Nolan. In seconds, Seamus muttered a complicated spell and threw a magickal bubble across the room, concealing Callum from the view of the crowd. For a moment, everyone looked around in confusion, and then a woman jumped up and ran to close the door. From outside the spell, it would look as though the group at the table continued to enjoy an easy-going conversation.

"Just the storm blowing the door open." Cait, owner of

Gallagher's Pub, shot Callum a look from where she manned the bar and the music commenced.

Thunder roared overhead, shaking the windows of the pub, and Cait ducked under the passthrough and went head-to-head with the Prince. Though she wasn't Fae, Cait had a magickal bloodline that fueled her confidence.

"That's enough of that now. You'll be replacing any windows you break." Cait's voice was low. Callum brushed her aside like she was a gnat and Bianca's swift hiss of breath was enough to assure Nolan that very few people were ballsy enough to treat Cait that way. Not to mention the fact that it was rare for Callum to be out-right rude.

Which meant something was very, very wrong.

He'd never seen the Prince like this before. In all the years he had stood by his side, both in battle and in overseeing the royal court of the Fae, Prince Callum lead with a cool head. Except when it came to his fated mate and one true love…Lily. The hair on the back of Nolan's neck lifted, as though darkness slithered over him, and his eyes held Callum's as the prince skidded to a stop at their table.

"Prince." Seamus bowed his head.

"Lily's missing." Callum's words fell like an icicle shattering to the ground.

Nolan was the first to speak.

"What happened? I can leave immediately. What should we do?"

Cait surprised Nolan by appearing at Callum's side once more, and she did something that no Fae would ever dare to do – she tugged Callum's hand until he was sitting on a chair in front of the table and handed him a whiskey.

"Tell us," Cait insisted.

Bianca's eyes darted to Nolan's, the pretty blonde having picked up on the break in Royal protocol, and he made a mental note that she might be useful for whatever lay before them. Because if something bad *had* happened – here in Grace's Cove and not in the Fae realm – well, they would need help navigating this world. Both Bianca and her husband, Seamus, had successfully supported the Seekers on their quest to save the Four Treasures from the Domnua, the evil fae, over two decades ago. It looked like they were about to be recruited for another quest.

Pulling his eyes back to the Prince, Nolan waited until Callum had swallowed the whiskey and then schooled his breathing. Outside their magickal bubble, the band played on and a few people had pushed chairs aside to throw themselves into a measure of complicated dance steps. Any other night, and Nolan would have joined them. When he was on duty – Nolan allowed nothing to distract him from the job. But, like all Fae, Nolan loved celebrations and where there was music, there'd often be Fae dancing just outside the awareness of humans.

"It's the Water Fae." Once more Callum leveled a fierce look at Nolan, and his insides twisted. The Water Fae were the faction of elemental Fae that Nolan commanded. It was his duty to oversee and manage their concerns and needs – which meant something, likely the Domnua, had forced the Water Fae to act out.

"You're certain?" Nolan asked, his words sharp.

"Aye, sure and I'm certain. Didn't they already try to kill me?"

It had come as a great surprise to everyone in the Fae

realm, particularly those in the Royal court, when the Water Fae had launched a surprise attack on Prince Callum, nearly drowning him on his mission to find his fated mate. Luckily, Callum had survived and had mated with his beautiful Lily, and Nolan had been left to clean up the mess with the Water Fae.

Which, he'd *thought* he'd handled…

"Sir, I met with the leader just this week."

"And what was the resolution of this meeting?"

"I met with the Water Fae on their turf – in their protected cave deep in the sea. I was quite confident that we'd left the meeting with a mutual respect and under-standing. They'd brought up some concerns for me to address, and I've already made good on one of them."

"Which one?" Callum asked, his fingers clenched tightly on the whiskey glass. The rest of the table remained silent, their eyes bouncing between Callum and Nolan like they were watching a tennis match.

"They desired that the path of the human's cargo ships be amended slightly as it crossed too closely to their nurseries in the kelp. I adjusted the currents of the ocean to force the boats to give a wider berth to that particular area." Nolan had been proud of this particular feat, as it had taken careful manage-ment of many natural elements, not to mention adjusting human behavior without them being aware of it. He'd also been pleased to be able to help the Water Fae quickly, so they would understand that he was working on behalf of them as a representative in the higher realms of Fae Court.

"And that's all? Nothing else…untoward happened in this meeting?"

Nolan was shocked by the note of suspicion in Callum's voice. Not only had Nolan proven his allegiance to the prince numerous times over, but they were also friends. The accusing look in his eyes sent a shiver across the back of Nolan's neck. While Callum was known for being fair, he could also be ruthless. If there was any reason for Callum to suspect that Nolan was involved in Lily's disappearance – he'd be dead before the end of the night.

"No, sir. It was one of our better meetings. Frankly, I'm surprised by this. I was quite pleased with the results of our negotiations, and it had sounded like the elders were as well. Please, can you tell me what happened?" Nolan took a careful sip of his whiskey, the liquid burning a hot trail to his stomach.

"I only left her for a moment." Callum's voice was ragged, his eyes haunted. "I'd promised her I was going to try to light a fire like humans do." Callum waved his hand in the air. "You know, with the wood, and the flame, and the tinder…all that nonsense. She wanted to see if I would have the patience to try it without my magick, you see. It was a game, really. We were having fun…laughing. I went outside into the storm to get the firewood from the shed. She'd…she'd been standing in the doorway, just a touch in the rain, laughing out at me because she wanted to watch me do manual labor."

Bianca looked as though she wanted to make a comment about if building a fire was really manual labor but shut her mouth when Seamus touched her arm briefly. The two worked beautifully together, and were so in tune that Nolan was surprised that Seamus had even had to physically correct her.

"When I came back...wood in my arms...she was gone." Callum slammed his fist down on the table and a flash of lightning lit the sky outside the pub. In seconds, thunder followed, shaking the room with its wrath. "The door was wide open. And...just this."

Callum pulled out a piece of parchment paper and put it on the table. Nolan leaned over, not touching it for Fae magick was tricky on an easy day – and read the words.

We trade a love for a love. You've stolen our power. Now we steal your heart.

Below the words was a sketch of a talisman etched with an intricate Celtic knot. It was a drawing of the Water Fae's amulet, which was unimaginably powerful in the wrong hands, and only worn by the leader of the Water Fae. Each faction of the elemental Fae had a ruling talisman such as the amulet, and the leader always had it on hand lest it be stolen and used for wrongdoing. Panic slipped through Nolan as he met Callum's eyes.

"The amulet. It's missing."

"Aye, and they think *we* stole it."

Song of the Fae

AFTERWORD

As always, thank you for joining me back in my favorite fictional town - Grace's Cove. While the town itself is modeled after beautiful Dingle, Ireland, located along the Wild Atlantic Way, the magick is all of my own making. Or is it? If you spend any time in Ireland you'll soon discover that there's magick of all kinds to be found - from ancient stone circles to a friendly smile from a pub owner. I know we are all looking for some magick in our lives right now, and I challenge you to go out and create your own. What an enchanting world we live in - you've only but to dream a little.

I hope my books have added a little magick into your life. If you have a moment to add some to my day, you can help by telling your friends and leaving a review. Word-of-mouth is the most powerful way to share my stories. Thank you.

Have you read books from my other series? Please join our little community by signing up for my newsletter. Use the link below for a welcome bonus - a free short story!

Niamh and Mac are at a turning point in their relationship. Mac knows what he wants, but will Niamh be able to accept it? Download this free short story and see if the cove will glow blue for their love.

"One Year Later"
… discover if he's ready to pop the big question or not!

www.triciaomalley.com/story

In January 2023 we will be returning to Grace's Cove in book 12 of the Mystic Cove series. Wild Irish Moon.

Available for pre-order now.

THE ISLE OF DESTINY SERIES

ALSO BY TRICIA O'MALLEY

Stone Song

Sword Song

Spear Song

Sphere Song

"Love this series. I will read this multiple times. Keeps you on the edge of your seat. It has action, excitement and romance all in one series."- Amazon Review

Available in audio, e-book & paperback!

Available Now

THE MYSTIC COVE SERIES

Wild Irish Heart

Wild Irish Eyes

Wild Irish Soul

Wild Irish Rebel

Wild Irish Roots: Margaret & Sean

Wild Irish Witch

Wild Irish Grace

Wild Irish Dreamer

Wild Irish Christmas (Novella)

Wild Irish Sage

Wild Irish Renegade

Wild Irish Moon

"I have read thousands of books and a fair percentage have been romances. Until I read Wild Irish Heart, I never had a book actually make me believe in love."- Amazon Review

Available in audio, e-book & paperback!

THE SIREN ISLAND SERIES

ALSO BY TRICIA O'MALLEY

Good Girl

Up to No Good

A Good Chance

Good Moon Rising

Too Good to Be True

A Good Soul

In Good Time

"Love her books and was excited for a totally new and different one! Once again, she did NOT disappoint! Magical in multiple ways and on multiple levels. Her writing style, while similar to that of Nora Roberts, kicks it up a notch!! I want to visit that island, stay in the B&B and meet the gals who run it! The characters are THAT real!!!" - Amazon Review

Available in audio, e-book & paperback!

THE ALTHEA ROSE SERIES

ALSO BY TRICIA O'MALLEY

One Tequila

Tequila for Two

Tequila Will Kill Ya (Novella)

Three Tequilas

Tequila Shots & Valentine Knots (Novella)

Tequila Four

A Fifth of Tequila

A Sixer of Tequila

Seven Deadly Tequilas

Eight Ways to Tequila

Tequila for Christmas (Novella)

"Not my usual genre but couldn't resist the Florida Keys setting. I was hooked from the first page. A fun read with just the right amount of crazy! Will definitely follow this series."- Amazon Review

Available in audio, e-book & paperback!

ALSO BY TRICIA O'MALLEY

STAND ALONE NOVELS

Ms. Bitch

"Ms. Bitch is sunshine in a book! An uplifting story of fighting your way through heartbreak and making your own version of happily-ever-after."

~Ann Charles, USA Today Bestselling Author

One Way Ticket

A funny and captivating beach read where booking a one-way ticket to paradise means starting over, letting go, and taking a chance on love…one more time

10 out of 10 - The BookLife Prize semi finalist

Firebird Award Winner

Pencraft Book of the year 2021

Made in United States
North Haven, CT
03 June 2022